Bed Change

A Nina Bannister Mystery

by

T'Gracie and Joe Reese

For information, email **Cozy Cat Press**, cozycatpress@aol.com or visit our website at: www.cozycatpress.com

COZY CAT
P R E S S

ISBN: 978-1-946063-31-1

Printed in the United States of America
Cover design by Paula Ellenberger
www.paulaellenberger.com
1 2 3 4 5 6 7 8 9 10

For Kitty "Furl"
1999-2017

CHAPTER ONE: GRAY AND GRAYER

January in Bay St. Lucy.
3:00 P.M.

Standing hip deep in sea water, the roar of surf behind her, rubber waders clinging to her legs, Nina Bannister cast one more time, then watched the red bobber do nothing very interesting except float aimlessly in the foam of a three foot wave.

She let her eyes roam along the horizon, noting that the sky and the sea had become precisely the same. She could discern no clouds in the ocean and no fish in the heavens; no, it was all one dreary mix, making her doubt the wisdom of living on the coast, and doubt equally the poetic sentiments that raved about the allure of the ever changing sea, the sea, down to the sea in boats, down to the…

…blah blah blah.

It was almost enough to make one wish for summer and its endless supply of tourists.

Of course it wasn't merely the weather that was depressing her. It was life in general. Christmas had been lonely. There were parties to go to, of course, but it seemed like every year there were fewer of them. Her friends from decades ago had died, or were in the process of dying, or were not quite sick enough to be dying yet, but soon would be, or were just too tired to go to all the trouble.

New Year's Eve she had spent alone.

Well, not really alone because there was always Furl.

Except that Furl did not really enjoy champagne, and the little round balls of excrement he continually left for her on the living room carpet did not really count as party favors.

She was cold. The bright yellow hip boots kept her feet and legs dry, and she had on every wool sweater she owned; but even if forty-seven degrees did not sound particularly cold for January, the wan disc that would have been beaming sun in July had simply run out of energy now, and it was no longer good at heating anything or growing anything.

Yes, she was cold.

And she wasn't catching any fish.

And if she did catch any fish, she didn't particularly feel like cooking them.

Or doing anything else for that matter.

She had always hated the thought that she might become a sad and lonely person as she grew older. It couldn't happen, not to her. No, she had gotten through the agonizing first year without Frank, had forced herself to be far more outgoing than the young Nina had ever been, had developed interests—painting, theatre, even politics—and she frequently found herself thinking just before she closed her eyes and drifted off to sleep, that she was a pretty lucky and happy little human being after all.

So what had changed?

Maybe she was just growing older.

The 'like to do' button on her soul had worn down, as had the 'look forward to' mechanism.

The bobber disappeared.

But darn it, one instant before she could give the rod that satisfactory jerk that was always followed by an exhilarating tug at the other end—it bobbed back up to the surface again.

Maybe the fish all felt like she did.

She slogged out of the surf and made her way back up the hard packed beach toward the Vespa that was, outside of herself, the only object apparent on the Mississippi Gulf Coast. No, check that: a pelican was sweeping along over the first breaking whitecaps some twenty yards out. But other than that, it could have been the end of the world or the beginning of it.

She forced herself to think of dinner.

What did she have in the house?

There was one microwaveable package of Dinty Moore's Beef Stew.

Not too exciting, that.

A can of Hormel Chili.

Same as the Dinty Moore Beef Stew on the excitement chart.

And then, come to think of it, who were these people? Who was Dinty Moore? And who was Hormel? Charles Hormel? Ludwig Hormel, from the Old Country?

Her kitchen was inundated with the names of strange people, and with canned products that could have been years old.

But one of those products, she realized with a sigh, would be inside her in an hour or so, unless she chose to make other plans. She could go to Beach Mart Supermarket, but she didn't quite have the energy to do that; or she could go out to eat. Pizza Hut. Arby's (the onion rings were always hot, and good). Mister Taco.

Was there a Mrs. Taco, or were they now living apart?

She reached the Vespa, unlocked it from the bicycle rack, wondering why she had bothered to lock it in the first place, took a faded yellow towel from the basket over the back wheel, and wiped it over the driver's seat, which had collected a thin layer of sand, blown by the north wind. She took her helmet from where she had left it hanging from the handle bar and fit it onto her head, snapping the strap under her chin. Her left leg pained her a bit as she got onto the machine, and she wondered if perhaps the long morning walks along the beach might need to be shortened a bit.

Engine starting now.

VROOOM VROOOM in many cars.

Puttputtputtputt in the Vespa.

She accelerated slowly over the dunes trail, dinner having left her mind now, replaced by disturbing memories of her earlier afternoon trip to the library. Her normal sanctuary, her church away from church, where she could always go for inspiration, comfort, mental stimulation, ideas—everything that made life worth living.

Except that this afternoon it had been dead to her, dead as this leaden sky and that colorless ocean out there.

She had walked past Jane Austin's place on the shelves without hearing or feeling anything. Perhaps there was a kind of limit on the number of times one might read *Northanger Abbey* and still respond to it. Thirteen did not seem too high a number, especially not when compared to *Emma*'s twenty three.

But perhaps it was.

It seemed, during the first minutes, that the answer might lie in genre or time period. Perhaps the nineteenth century was not appropriate for this wintry Mississippi climate. Perhaps the standard good old mysteries might be better. But as she passed them on the shelves, much as one might pass the houses of good old friends on a quiet residential street, she found their windows shuttered and their doors locked.

Agatha Christie was simply not at home to her. Nor Dorothy Sayers. Nor P.D. James. Nor even Janet Evanovich.

She did not, ultimately, care who did it, and if it was or wasn't the butler or the long disappeared and yet still embittered late aunt, what did it matter?

In fact there was only one book in the library that spoke to her at all.

She approached it, took it off the shelf, and watched as it fell magically to one play, one scene, one passage.

And there he stood before her, a bit dust covered, but still eloquent, and still chilling, Hamlet, as he looked into her Nina Bannister soul and said coldly:

'How weary, dull, stale and flat, seem to me all the uses of this world.'

She had tried to pretend that the words did not apply to her.

No, she had not lost her love of books.

That simply could not happen.

Banish books?

One might as leave say, if still in a Shakespeare mood:

'Banish Falstaff and banish life!'

But for now they might as well have been banished, so uninteresting were they to her.

So, her left leg still bothering her a bit, she hobbled out of the library.

All of that had happened hours ago, before the ill-fated attempt at fishing. It was getting dark now—six fifteen—and a cold dirty rain was beginning to fall. She entered the downtown area of Bay St. Lucy. Lights glared around her. Filling stations, restaurants—and there, in front of her and just to the right, the store she feared most.

It seemed to pull the Vespa toward its rain-glistening parking lot.

No, Nina, don't let yourself be pulled in there.

And now she was abreast of the sign, glaring red in the rain, circular, festive.

"Old Mister Pelican's Discount Liquor."

Where she could get wine. Not too much. Not an extra-large bottle. Just one little elegant bottle of Shiraz. Or Cabernet Sauvignon. Or Merlot. Not a white wine, for cold white wine meant summer. But a hearty red, which would make even the Dinty Moore Beef Stew seem a succulent repast. One bottle. And, of course, she would not drink even half of that. A glass, and nothing more. A glass to stimulate her appetite and take the edge of the somber and even grueling thing that this depressing day had been.

One glass.

Not much money for the bottle. Seven dollars? Eight? Surely she could afford that.

Turn in! Turn in here, Nina!

But she did not.

And now the red flashing sign was disappearing in her rear view mirror.

Good bye and good riddance, liquor store.

Because she knew what would happen.

One glass would turn into two, and there she would be, doing the one thing she knew might lead to disaster.

Drinking alone.

If she had been depressed anyway, at least it was a sober depression.

She might be a melancholic and a solitary embittered old woman.

But she would not let herself turn into a drunk.

And the store's sign had disappeared from the rear view mirror.

Three minutes later she was home. She pulled the Vespa carefully between two of the stork-leg poles upon which her seaside shack rested, she turned off the engine, and she looked around, letting her eye scan the walls of what served as her open garage. Fishnets, poles, articles of clothing, hoes, garden tools (and, yes, she would someday find a method of raising tomatoes in air half-filled with sand and soil caked with ocean brine), and there, ten feet from her front bumper, the charcoal broiler which she had decided never to use during winter months, more as an offering to The Gods of Four Seasons, than as an admission of fear of Mississippi cold.

She got off the cycle.

Damned leg.

A bath. A hot bath. Maybe a little muscle relaxant, and certainly an Advil. Wine was unacceptable, but not medicine. If she felt depressed anyway, then the last thing she needed was a sleepless night, tossing around in bed and thinking about this and that.

No, she decided, taking off the big yellow oilcloth overcoat and hanging it in its accustomed place. There was no telling what else she would do tonight—she had hated television for decades now and had no set in her house or ever would until they stopped showing video games and talk shows and went back to only the movies of James Stewart and June Allyson—but taking a bath was definitely high on the list.

Now the waders came off, and now the galoshes.

So that, clad in only a light jacket, two sweaters, a pair of faded jeans, and some ragged tennis shoes, she went outside in the cold rain, walked up the rickety stairs, inserted the key in the lock—and entered her—

—her what?

People were always telling her to call it a flat or a bungalow, but it was a shack, so why not call it that?

She entered her shack.

Furl, who had been lying in front of the couch, growled ill-naturedly at her.

She, noting the two spherical dull brown presents he had left for her beside the big green chair, growled back, equally ill-naturedly.

She made her way into the pantry, took a package of cat food from a lower shelf, bent, and poured a dozen or so granules of dry Furl Fodder into the dish.

"There you go. So tell me: what useful things did you do today to earn your room and board?"

Furl did not answer, intent as he was upon nosing, examining, evaluating, and finally grudgingly eating, his dinner.

She watched him for a time, noting with equal degrees of pride and depression that feeding this animal was the only useful thing she had done all day.

Then she went into the bedroom, peeled off the outer sweater, which was blue, the middle sweater, which was green, and the inner sweater, which had no color at all.

Rain was beginning to patter upon the tin roof of the bung—of the shack, and a north wind was beginning to howl.

She sat on the bed, asking herself, finally out loud:

"What am I going to do tonight?"

Then she pulled off her left tennis shoe.

She sat for a time, gazing at her partially white sock covered left foot.

The ankle—and much of the foot—was hugely swollen.

There was no foot at all. There were no contours, no bones, no veins, no muscles.

Only a pasty white something that resembled bloodless skin, elephantine, insensitive to touch, and twice the size of her own old regular foot.

"My God," she heard herself whispering.

"My God—what's happened to me?"

And so she sat and stared, hoping this was a dream.

But it was no dream, and the monstrous ugly bloated thing that had been bursting out of her shoe remained as it was.

It was all too horrible.

Except there was one bit of perverse humor about it.

One thing that made her almost smile as it crossed her mind.

It was even worth saying aloud, since it was not 'My God.'

And so she said it:

"At least I know what I'll do tonight."

And she did.

CHAPTER TWO: A THING TO DO, A PLACE TO GO

The hospital loomed before her, immense, dark, resembling more a giant tomb than a place of healing. There could not have been, she found herself thinking, too many patients in the place, for it usually housed summer tourists who had sunbathed too much or eaten too much or drunk too much or simply done unwise things on vacation that they never would have attempted back home in Iowa.

There was one glowing red spot of light, which looked as though it could have served to advertise Mr. Burger or a fried chicken joint. The only difference was that, instead of announcing steak and fries with a malted thrown in all for less than five dollars, it said simply: EMERGENCY.

Was this an emergency?

Her foot/ankle did not hurt. She could walk on it. Perhaps she should simply wait until morning.

One good night's sleep and the whole thing would be a memory. She would wake up, feed Furl, and look down at a perfectly normal appendage. It would all have been made right again by the magic of slumber. Then later in the morning she would drive along Sand Dollar Way and park in the little lot belonging to her regular doctor, Dr. Morgan.

He would 'work her in,' as he always did when she had various unexplained aches and pains, and he would explain to her what had caused this thing (It happens quite frequently—it's nothing to worry about, just stay off it for a day or so.)

And that would be that.

So thinking she bent forward, pulled back her sock, and winced at the thing before her, which appeared to be not a foot at all but a badly made massive cast encircling a foot.

"No," she whispered.

Whatever this was, it needed looking after.

Now.

And so she took off her helmet and put on her blue floppy rain hat, pushed the kick stand down and got off.

The glaring red sign, as she made her way toward it, seemed to make her hungry.

I'll have a number two please, she found herself wanting to say instead of:

Why does my ankle look like an elephant's ankle?

Pondering these thoughts, she made her way into the emergency room.

It was empty, save for a great many copies of *People Magazine* and *Field and Stream*, and a young woman who looked as though she could have been an airline stewardess, sitting behind the reception desk.

The stewardess straightened, closed the smart phone on which she had been texting, put it in a drawer beside her, closed the drawer, and then smiled her obligatory smile, chirping out her obligatory greeting:

"Good evening, ma'am."

"Good evening. My name is Nina Bannister."

"And what seems to be the nature of your problem, Ms. Bannister?"

"My ankle is swollen."

"Oh, that's too bad. Did you twist it or sprain it?"

"No, that's the problem. I didn't do anything to it. I just looked at it half an hour ago, after I got in from fishing—and it's huge."

"Were you fishing out in the surf?"

"Yes, I do that often, even in the winter."

"Could something have stung you? A sting ray?"

"I don't think so. I would have felt it. But my ankle doesn't hurt."

"I see. You say you aren't in pain at the moment?"

"No."

"Then could you possibly have a seat here at the counter and answer a few questions for me? Also there are some papers you need to scan and sign."

"Of course."

Nina sat down, looking at an ominous pile of papers that seemed to appear by magic on the counter by her right arm.

"Now, Ms. Bannister—do you have insurance?"

"Yes, Medicare and Gerber Plan B Supplement."

"All right, if I could see the cards—"

Nina showed her the cards.

"Good. Now if I could have the last 4 digits of your social—"

"4 1 3 5."

"Excellent. Your birthday?"

"9-15-46."

"And, if you'd write your relevant information on this top sheet—"

Nina did so, wondering who would do these things if she were in agonizing pain.

Name. Address. Social Security number. Again.

And diseases.

Had she suffered from—

Dyspepsia Heart Disease Mumps Kidney Failure Trouble Breathing Cancer Gout High Blood Pressure—

She kept checking 'no' in the little boxes, but, as she did so, she could feel herself forgetting the foot and feeling deathly sick with hundreds of bizarre illnesses she had never really suffered from.

Glaucoma
Skin Cancer
Hypertension
Shingles.
No no no no
Rheumatoid Arthritis.

After five minutes of this—but it seemed an eternity—she pushed the completed stack of documents back to the receptionist, who asked:

"What is your birthday?"

"9-15-46," she repeated.

The receptionist scanned the documents and nodded approvingly, except for the moment she frowned and asked:

"In the line marked 'Contact information' here—"

"Yes?"

"You've written 'Furl.'"

"Furl is my cat."

"I think they need a human."

She wrote 'Alanna Delafosse,' wondering what was wrong with 'Furl.'

After this, she was consigned to the bowels of the waiting room, where she chose between Jenn's new romance and stalking elk in southern Vermont. Neither read seemed particularly compelling, so she merely sat there with part of her mind on the foot, and part on the depression that had clouded over this already leaden-cloudy day. Here, sitting in the gigantic hospital, it seemed worse. She was sick, something was wrong with her, and she had no idea what it could be. But worse than being sick was being sick alone. She had no one to drive her to the emergency room, no one to go by the shack and get her some things, should she be forced to stay overnight—or longer—in the hospital. She had written 'Furl' as her contact, and, shocking as it was, she had not done this as a joke.

"Ms. Bannister?" asked the receptionist across the room, who seemed to be scanning the documents one last time:

"Yes?"

"Your birthday?"

"9-15-46."

"Thank you."

A gun. If she could only have a gun—

But that would not help.

Her friends were disappearing.

She tried having an imaginary conversation with Frank, and even that did not work. She had nothing to say to the ghost of her long dead husband.

She had nothing to say to anybody.

No one here knew her.

No one could come and…

"Nina!"

At this moment, the door on the far side of the waiting room burst open and a force of nature nurse burst open with it, almost springing into the room and grinning broadly as she announced:

"As I live and breathe—it's Nina Bannister!"

That much at least was right, Nina found herself thinking. But who was this nearly six foot tall chunk of part flesh part nuclear energy, blonde ringlets clutching tight to her scalp, muscular arms held out as though ready for an embrace, despite the twenty foot distance between herself and the chair in which Nina was seated?

Who *was* this?

"Don't recognize me?"

The only possible answer to this was 'no,' but Nina was too embarrassed to say it, and so she, as clearly as possible, said:

"Uuuuhhhh—"

"Bridget O'Leary! 'Bridge' to everybody in our home room that year. 'Bridge because I'm so tall! Bridge over all the girls in the class and half the boys!"

This girl, this girl—

—so many students. Thirty years of being principal. So many students—

—yes! There she was, pulled up from the musty memory files! An outrageous girl, laughing all the time and causing trouble.

What had ever happened to—

—oh yes. THAT had happened to her. Pregnant as a sixteen year old junior. When was that? Fifteen years ago. Pregnant and kicked out of school. So how had she managed to…

"I've been here a year now as a head nurse after ten years at a hospital in Meridian. I've been meaning to come by and see you, Ms. Bannister. I hear you retired."

"Yes. Ten years ago."

"I'm sorry to hear that. You were so great as principal. If anybody deserves to have a good retirement, though, it's you. And I'm sorry I haven't looked you up."

"You haven't had time, Bridget. You've been curing people."

"Not all of them. But maybe we help some. I just have to tell you though. You were the best teacher I ever had. And the best principal. The very best. When that thing happened with my baby, you were the only one on the administration who really fought for me. I had to leave school—but you did everything you could to fight for me."

"And you had the baby, which—I remember now— you named Jeremy."

The smile broadened:

"Yes, ma'am. Then I got my GED and then, somehow, got into nursing school. I'm not sure I could have done it without you."

"But I didn't do anything to help you, Bridget!"

"Yes, you did! It's what you taught us! You were not just the principal when I got to high school—you taught English, too, and showed us movies. There's one I'll never forget: *Mildred Pierce*."

"Oh yes! I do remember showing that—Joan Crawford."

"And Joan wouldn't quit. No matter what happened—she wouldn't quit. And every time I even thought about quitting, I thought of her. I'm not alone, Ms. Bannister—everybody thought you were great. But that's enough for now. What's wrong with you, Ms. Bannister? Why are you here in Emergency?"

"Well, first, let's have no more of the Ms. Bannister stuff. It's Nina."

"All right then, Nina. What seems to be the problem?"

"My ankle and foot. They're swollen up. Huge."

"You didn't fall on them or sprain them?"

"No. I was out in the surf fishing, in big rubber boots. When I got back home to take my clothes off so that I could shower, I saw that my foot had swollen."

"Did it hurt?"

"No."

"Does it hurt now?"

"No, there's no pain at all—but when I touch that doughy swollen flesh, I can't feel anything."

"All right. First thing to do is get you into an examination room. Here, you come along with me."

She led Nina through a doorway beyond which opened a network of hallways. Upon the walls of each narrow hall—all of them painted some color between beige and yellow—hung paintings of human organs, below which were stenciled such phrases as:

"The Seven Warning Signs of Liver Cancer"

Or—

"The Effective Prevention of Hepatitis C"

Nina averted her eyes and attempted simply to follow the directions of Bridget, who stayed close behind her.

"We're gonna turn left here, Nina. Now right."

Finally, they stood before a small room that Nina assumed was to be hers.

"Still no pain?"

"No," she answered.

But then she remembered:

"There is one thing."

"What?"

"My leg has been sore the last few days."

"Left leg?"

"Yes."

"Sure you didn't pull it jogging or something like that?"

"Pretty certain. I sometimes jog on the beach but not last week."

"Sharp pain?"

"Dull ache."

"All right. Have a seat on the end of this examination table, slip off your tennis shoe and roll up your pants leg.

Never before had Nina so longed to be made a fool of. The shoe would come off, the pants leg would be rolled up—and voila—nothing wrong! The same old Bannister foot and ankle construction, bones just as normal, tendons and ligaments streaking here and there, linking toes and calf.

A false alarm!

They would laugh about it and Nina would go home.

Home to Furl and bed.

And so the shoe came off. The pants leg went up.

And there, spreading itself out in sickly white and massive proportions, was the thing she had seen in her bedroom.

She looked at it with horror; Bridget looked at it with cool lack of passion, and the experienced eye of the professional.

"How long has it been like this?"

"A couple of hours, I suppose. It wasn't like this when I went in fishing."

"And that was?"

"About two thirty."

"So this swelling happened within the space of two or three hours?"

'About that."

"Nina, I'm certain the doctor is going to want to take a look at this. I'm also certain there will be a couple of tests. You'd better get out of those sweaters and jeans and into a hospital gown. And while you do that, I'll put a call in for the doctor and alert the lab."

So saying, she reached into a drawer beside her, withdrew what looked like a yellow pillowcase with button and a drawstring, handed it to Nina, and left the room.

Nina stood up, peeled off two sweaters, which she hung on the back of a facing chair, then took off her pants and socks.

She had never felt so utterly naked in her life, although she still had on her undergarments.

Would they want her to remove those, too?

She held up the pillowcase/hospital gown, slipped her arms through the two openings, and began to tie two cords in front of her.

She had done the first knot and the door opened again, revealing Bridgett and a second nurse, tall and

willowy, equally overjoyed, it seemed, to see Nina in
the emergency room.

"Ms. Bannister!"

And this one—thank heaven, she found herself
thinking—Nina knew.

"Latricia Smith!"

"Our coach! Our great old coach! The Hattiesburg
game!"

"Latricia, what are you doing here?"

"Just like Bridget, I'm a nurse! And just like her,
I've only been back in Bay St. Lucy for little more than
a year."

"You scored seven points in the Hattiesburg game!"

"You remember?"

"I remember every little detail of that game, and
never will forget it."

"Me neither! I was so proud! We all were! So what's
wrong with you, Coach?"

"Well, I—"

Bridget interrupted, while carefully steering into the
room a clattering metal table, behind which stood
another metallic device, the one for measuring blood
pressure, Nina assumed, and the other for the extraction
of blood itself.

"We don't know what's wrong with her. We're
going to find out though. After we show her how to put
the gown on."

"What's wrong," asked Nina, "with the way I put the
gown on?"

"You've got it backwards. It ties in the back."

"The back? How can I tic it back there? I can't reach
back there—I was doing good to get it tied out here in
the front."

"You can get it tied back there because you have two
students willing to help you. Here—take it off and let's
get it turned around."

Both of the two women worked at shucking Nina out of the impossible garment and shucking her into it the proper way, leaving Nina to wonder how anyone would have tied the thing properly without part of a medical staff to intervene.

She looked down at the thing, hanging featureless and buttonless in front of her.

"I look like a butcher," she said, quietly.

Bridget did not reply to this, but merely opened the door and said:

"Here's the doctor."

A slight, and quiet young, Nina thought, woman entered the room.

She looked like a scaled down version of Omar Sharif, if Omar Sharif had been a woman, and garbed in the pale blue uniform of a surgeon. But those things did not matter: she had the dark bottomless eyes of the soul of India, and her seamless voice poured into the small room like the Ganges itself:

"You are Ms. Bannister, I believe?"

"Yes, I'm Nina Bannister."

"So very good to know you. I am Dr. Singh, Lalima Singh."

"It's good to meet you, Dr. Singh."

"I have, of course, heard of you, Ms. Bannister. As who has not? I was just finishing up my studies in New Delhi when word came of the great march on Washington. The Lysistrata movement which you organized. I was part of a similar attempt in New Delhi itself. India, whether you know it or not, is even worse than your country. It is a very sexist country, a very sexist culture. Ten years ago I would never have been considered for medical school, so there has been progress. But it is as you said in that so eventful summer: we outnumber them, the men, so why do we let them tell us what we must do?"

The doctor glanced at a chart she was holding, then sat on a high stool beside the table upon which Nina lay.

"Some good was done though. Some legislative seats were gained, both in this country and in mine. The work must continue though."

"Yes," said Nina, "that's true."

"So, are you organizing another 'Lissie' movement?"

"No, I think others have taken on that role. I'm pretty much retired from politics now."

"I see. Well, you have certainly earned the right to step back from the battle. But, if you do not mind, I should like to speak more with you in the future and learn about how you did it. I want to be like you, and to be active in organizational matters. Would that be all right?"

"Of course."

"Good! Then, until later."

So saying, she shook Nina's hand, turned around in a businesslike matter, and left.

There was silence in the room except for the dull growl of air conditioning and the wail of a siren approaching from downtown. The room was the temperature of an ice chest. Nina shivered, which was noticed by Bridget. "Are you cold, Ms. Bannister? Here, let me get you a blanket," she said, reaching into a closet for a thin hospital blanket and handing it to Nina.

"Thanks, Bridget, sometimes I think I'm colder inside in the summer than outside in the winter."

"I know! It's so air conditioned, even in winter, that we blame the surgeons."

Finally, Nina said:

"She didn't say anything about my foot."

Bridget shook her head:

"No. But I have to tell you, Nina, she's right about the 'Lissie' movement. I've got to say, it inspired me. It seemed like the cards were stacked against me, that the laws had all been written for the men and by the men. If I hadn't remembered you as a teacher, and thought of all the things you had told us, showed us—"

"Yes, but my foot—"

Another figure appeared in the doorway, this one a tall blonde gangly young man.

He smiled and said:

"Hello, Ms. Bannister! I'm Larry Ewing!"

"Larry—"

"I got caught smoking pot in the eleventh grade. They were going to kick me out of school and maybe put me in jail—but somehow you talked to Officer Rivard and all I had to do was stay in the library an hour after school was out for two weeks."

How in the world, Nina asked herself, had she managed to do that?

Probably because, if truth be known, Moon Rivard had smoked a bit of pot when he himself was in the eleventh grade.

"Anyway, I'm still grateful to you. Now if you can hop down off the table and lie on this stretcher, I'll take you up to the lab."

Nina hopped as well as she could from the table, wobbled over to the stretcher upon which she assumed she would be wheeled through the halls of the hospital, and lay down upon it, asking the grinning young man who was now to take charge of her:

"You don't still smoke marijuana, do you?"

Laughter from Bridget, laughter from Larry Ewing, who said:

"No, ma'am! Not for a long time!"

"I'm so glad to hear that. I'm glad I was able to keep you out of jail. And Bridget?"

"Yes, Nina?"

"Bridget, I'm glad the Lissie movement helped you. I'm glad it helped Dr. Singh. I'm glad Mildred Pierce inspired you. But could you just tell me where the hell I'm going?"

"Oh, Larry's just going to wheel you up to the lab. The doctor's ordered an MRI on you."

And with that, she found herself wheeled out into the hospital.

She lay for a time as still as possible, palms lying on naval, eyes fixed on the antiseptic ceiling as the cart she was lying on passed beneath large circular glaring lights. She tried not to think about anything at all, but she failed. She thought about her foot and ankle, and wondered what grotesque disease had made them swell up so. She thought about tonight and the next night and the next. A scant two hours ago she was feeling bored at the prospect of a night along in the shack. That would have been bad enough. But now? Now, gowned and test ready as she was, she was certainly going to have to spend the night here in the hospital. Alone. Hospital food to eat.

Who would take care of Furl?

She hated hospitals. Antiseptic places that they were.

And the words came back to her as she clattered down one hall, turned into another, then was wheeled into an elevator. The words—

Alone, alone, all all alone, alone on a wide wide sea.

But then the elevator door opened, revealing a small mob of light blue clad nurses and orderlies, all of whom surrounded the stretcher, all of whom had somehow been informed of her presence here:

"Ms. Bannister, I'm Margo! You taught us *The Great Gatsby* my sophomore year!"

"Ms. Bannister, I'm Tod Martel! You kept me from getting thrown out of school my junior year."

"Ms. Bannister, I'm Judy Denf. You wrote the recommendation that got me into Gulf State Junior College! I went on into their nursing program!"

"Ms. Bannister, remember me? Tom Darby! I had a car accident when I was fifteen and they said I had been drinking. Well, actually I had been drinking but you came late at night down to the police station and somehow got Officer Rivard to let me go home."

"Ms. Bannister—"

"Ms. Bannister—"

"Ms. Bannister—"

"Ms. Bannister—"

Good Lord, she found herself thinking. The whole Bay St. Lucy Hospital had been in her classroom at one time or another. And, had it not been for her, half of the people who were now caring for her would have been in some penitentiary.

The small parade continued on, higher and higher from ward to hallway to lab to larger lab, as the crowd grew gradually and the laughter increased, and more and more memories floated out into the dyspeptic atmosphere.

Finally, they came to a pair of large swinging doors. They stopped short, so that the entourage could promise a room visit just as soon as they all knew where their favorite teacher of all times was to be housed for the night.

Then the front bar of the stretcher pushed hard against the heavy metal doors, forcing them open.

She was about to get an MRI.

What, she wondered, was an MRI?

The room into which she now found herself pushed was larger than the examination room had been, and darker. It was in fact a fossil forest inhabited by great angular metallic med-tech dinosaurs which loomed up around her, frozen and motionless now but easily able to come menacingly to life at any time.

An older nurse that (she was almost forced to admit being glad about it) Nina had not taught, said in a low and dusky voice:

"So you're the famous Nina Bannister. Everyone in the hospital is talking about your being here."

"I've been here a little over an hour. How do they all know I'm here?"

A smile:

"A hospital is like a small town. It's more like a small town than a small town is. Apparently you're Bay St. Lucy's favorite teacher/principal and have been for many years.

"I was at it a long time."

"You must have been. So what's the matter with you?"

"I have a swollen foot."

"So I'm told. And you need an MRI. Well, let's get you one. Does it hurt to walk?"

"No."

"Then climb down from that stretcher and get up on this table. Once you're up here, we need you to lie on your—what foot is swollen?"

"Left."

"All right, then lie down on your right side. I'm going to put some oil on you, then run a silver metal disc up and down your side, from your armpit down your ribs and on farther to your knee. It won't hurt, but it might be cold. Come on over here now."

Nina did as she was told, wondering how many different modes of transference she would be carted onto and off of before this evening was done.

"Good. You want a blanket? You're shivering a little."

"Yes, that would be good."

The light blanket came, was draped over her, and was in fact good.

"You can curl up like a sow bug if you want. A lot of people do that."

There was a good deal of adjusting the massive machine beside her, and finally she winced slightly as the cold cream was spread in a narrow trail down her curled body. Then came the metal, and more wincing.

At least, she told herself, it wasn't a shot.

After a few minutes of this, the nurse said:

"Almost through now. In fact I think I'm going to buzz for Mr. Ewing to come back in. If they have your room ready, he can take you straight there and you won't have to go back to the examination room."

"What did you find?"

"You have a swollen foot."

"It takes all these machines to figure that out?"

"I know, seems a waste of time and space, doesn't it?"

"You're not going to tell me what's wrong with me, are you?"

"That's the doctor's job, Ms. Bannister. I'm just a flunky. Okay, down you go and over to the stretcher."

The transfer was made again and soon Nina was being wheeled back through the bowels of the hospital, toward the bed in which she was to spend the night. In a barren room, probably shared with an old complaining woman who snored or a young complaining woman who watched game shows on television.

No matter. The main thing was to accept this thing that was happening to her as an adventure, or, if not that, a challenge.

"Here we are, Ms. Bannister: Room 312. In we go."

And there, laid out before her, was all the herbage of the Indies. Plants galore, green plants, plants hanging from portable metal frames on which various machines once hung, flowers red yellow pink white…a sick-room greenhouse, dark green and ivy-strewn, blooming there on the third floor of what she had first thought of as a mausoleum.

Bridget appeared somehow, as though stepping out of the Congo, and said:

"They've been pouring in for the last hour, all these plants."

"This is amazing."

"Now come on, Ms. Bannister, let's get you into this bed."

And so once again, for what seemed the hundredth time, Nina was hauled from one piece of hospital furniture to another.

"Now I have to run this IV into your arm—"

Prick. Sting. Clear liquid going into arm from bag hanging above bed. A small tube running from the bag to the needle felt cool against Nina's arm.

"Does that feel okay where it's going into your arm?"

"It's fine."

"Good. Now we have to get you fed. It's a little late, but I think I can get the kitchen to send something up. I don't know if…"

"'Scuse me, mes amis!"

This from a short, stocky, curly-headed grinning figure who had just made his way inside the doorway:

Moon Rivard, police chief of Bay St. Lucy.

"Sorry to disturb you, Ms. Bannister—but I was kind of sent up here by your neighbors."

"Why, Moon? What's going on?"

"Crowd downstairs. They all waitin' outside, can't come in cause the hospital say no more visiting hours. But they must be forty or fifty folk wants to come in and tell you you sposed to get well."

"I can't believe it."

"You believe it, Ms. Bannister—it's happening. But here, I brought you these things."

He walked to the bed and handed her the small overnight travelling case that she had used somewhat frequently in past years.

"Folks started calling me when they heard you was here. I told 'em I didn't know what was wrong with you, but sometimes people b'lieve the police knows everything. Anyway, I got to talking with a lot of them, specially some ladies from the Methodist Church. We decided we'd all go over to your house, and maybe I could let 'em in, get some things that you might need. Maybe feed the cat, too. So we met up there. I fed the cat and they got these things together out of your bedroom and bathroom. Toothbrush and—you know, bath things, ladies' things."

"Thank you, Moon. And please thank them."

"Yes, ma'am, I will."

"How did you get in? Did you pick the lock? I'm told police know how to do that."

"No I didn't pick no lock."

"Do you have some kind of key that opens all—"

"You done left the door open, Ms. Bannister. Just hanging there, swinging a little in the breeze."

"Oh. Well. I guess I wasn't really thinking that well."

"Guess not. Anyway, I managed to get it locked and—well, here's your things."

The overnight case was taken by a pair of hands, which were replaced by another pair of hands, which held toward her a small brown grocery sack.

"Hey, Ms. Bannister, it's Julie. I talked with you a little while ago when you came in."

"Of course, Julie, what have you got there?"

"Something that's not supposed to be here in the hospital."

"What is it? Heroin?"

"It's kind of liquid heroin. You can't really have it while you're in here. But we're going to leave it in a special place downstairs, where nobody can find it. Then, when you get out, you can take it home with you—and maybe remember us when you open it."

Nina reached into the brown paper sack, pulled out the bottle, and read the label softly:

"Chateau Margot. 1969."

"It's supposed to be very good red wine."

"Yes. Yes, it is very good red wine. But you really should never have—"

"It's all right. A lot of us went in together on it. It was the best they had at Old Mr. Pelican's Liquor Store."

"If it's the best of Old Mr. Pelican," she said, "then it's the best in the world. Thank you so much!"

"You're welcome. Now just forget it exists, until you check out. We'll make sure you get it."

A moment's silence. Then a smaller figure, Dr. Lalima Singh, entered the room and said, quietly:

"It looks like an Indian rain forest. A beautiful thing indeed. But now the two of you should probably go. The patient needs her rest."

And finally Nina was alone with the doctor who said, looking at the now empty doorway:

"You have so many friends, Ms. Bannister."

Nina felt like crying but found herself laughing.

Sun-rain.

When she thought of all the people—

—all the people she had taught—

—all the wonderful people of Bay St. Lucy—

She stopped crying.

Now she was only laughing.

While Dr. Lalima Singh said quietly:

"And you also have a blood clot."

"Who cares?" said Nina.
And she went on laughing.

CHAPTER THREE: MEDICAL SCHOOL

The room was in dim light. The sun had set some time ago, and lights in the parking lot glowed like large planets, their images blurred by rain spattering against the windows.

"What does this mean?" Nina heard herself asking. "Why would a blood clot make my ankle and foot swell like this?"

Dr. Singh pulled a straight chair close to the bed upon which Nina was lying, smiled, and spoke softly, as though she were lecturing a group of students:

"The technical name for your swelling is Thrombophlebitis. This is a vein inflammation that is nearly in all cases—and definitely in yours, as the MRI revealed—caused by a blood clot. It typically occurs in the legs. A blood clot is a solid formation of blood cells that clump together. Blood clots can interfere with the normal flow of blood throughout the body; therefore they can, in some cases, be quite dangerous. Thrombophlebitis can occur in veins near the surface of your skin or deeper down between the muscle layers."

"How dangerous is my clot?"

Another smile:

"Not terribly, at least not in my opinion. You see, Ms. Bannister, there are two types of thrombophlebitis, deep vein and superficial. The first occurs when the clot takes place, as you can tell by the name, deep down in the body. Your case is definitely of the superficial variety. The clot is quite close to the surface. A strange thing: in your case the swelling, the thrombophlebitis, is probably a fortunate thing. The swelling itself is not dangerous, but it has called our attention to the clot, which we now can treat rather easily. Had the swelling not occurred, you might not have known about the clot, and it could have gone deeper into your leg, or even led to a pulmonary embolism."

"So how do we treat it?"

"The main thing we wish to do is keep you off the leg. Then we medicate you with blood thinners. The medication most frequently used, and which we shall use, is called Warfarin. You take it orally, two times per day. Tonight we shall hook you to an IV and pump a stronger blood thinner into your arm, so that, I hope at least, we shall see diminished swelling in the foot by tomorrow morning."

"How long do I have to stay in the hospital?"

A shake of the head:

"I think probably no longer than tonight. We shall see what the condition looks like around lunch tomorrow, but there is every chance you can go home. You will want to do two things: keep off the foot as far as any long walks or jogging, but do not let the foot be completely motionless for long periods of time. No long automobile trips or airline journeys."

"No, none of those planned."

"All right, then," said the doctor, standing up and taking a step toward the door. "I am working the late shift tonight, so I can check on you off and on through the evening."

She left the room, only to be replaced within minutes by an orderly pushing a rattling sliver cart upon which lay a chrome-covered food platter.

The orderly beamed more broadly, lifting the lid of the platter and revealing a huge red mass that could have been a human brain after a massive hemorrhage.

"Chicken breast with barbeque sauce," he said.

"With rice and a little salad?"

"Yes, ma'am."

"Wonderful! Thanks so much for bringing it up."

"No problem. That's a rolling cart that the platter is sitting on. Just push it away when you've finished. Someone will be up later tonight to collect it."

"I understand."

"Well, I'll leave you now. Enjoy your dinner, and have a restful night. It's after visiting hours so you shouldn't be bothered.

"Thank you so much."

And she was left alone.

Her first order of business was to deal with the food. She hid the mutant chicken breast as best as she could with two large napkins, then munched on rice and lightly oiled lettuce until she was no longer hungry.

Then she pushed the food cart over as far toward the wall as she could manage, wondering vaguely what she was going to do when she had to go to the bathroom. She looked down at the floor beneath her pillow and saw that the IV container hung from a rack that was on wheels. Clearly she would have to climb down from the bed and push the rack before her.

Well, she did not have to go to the bathroom now.

The problem would be solved when the problem actually arose.

Finally, she let her eye scan the side of the room itself.

Flowers, flowers, a hothouse, a tropical jungle of flowers. White red pink purple azaleas mums roses chrysanthemums and—what was that flower in the corner?

She didn't even recognize it.

And cards.

The hospital staff had left the cards pinned to the flower pots, so she could ultimately tell who had left what, but even from here she could see the images: lighthouses, boats, hearts.

She wanted to read the cards.

Did she dare try to get out of bed, roll the apparatus over to the wall, and read a few of them?

It would be practice for the more serious matter of going to the bathroom.

All right then! Legs up and out of the bed, then…

"Nina? Can I come in?"

Standing there in the doorway, a bit hunched over, a bit guilty-looking, more than a bit disheveled (but of course, this was normal for him) stood Tom Broussard.

"Tom?"

"Nina, how are you?"

"I'm fine—but what are you doing here? They just told me visiting hours are over!"

"Well, they're supposed to be, but I kind of talked Liz into letting me in anyway."

"Liz?"

"She's the receptionist."

"Oh yes, I remember. The one who kept giving me all those forms to fill out."

"Yeah, that's her."

"Do you know her?"

"We were kind of close before Penn and I got married."

"You were dating?"

"Actually we were—"

"That's all right; you don't need to go deeper into the matter. But again—what are you doing here?"

"I'm visiting you. Which is what the forty or so people down on the lawn below are trying to do, but the hospital won't let them in."

"There are forty people down there?"

"At least. Everybody knows you're in the hospital, but nobody knows exactly why. Some people say you had a heart attack and others say you were in a traffic accident on your Vespa."

"Neither of those things is true."

"What is true then?"

"I have a blood clot."

"Oh my God. Aren't you supposed to be in intensive care or something?"

"No, it's not that bad."

"Are you in pain?"

"No, I'm fine. Go back down there and tell everybody to go home. I mean, I appreciate their support, but it's really no big deal. The clot caused some swelling around my foot but the doctor says just stay off it and take blood thinner. I can probably go home tomorrow."

"That's great to hear, Nina. We all thought we were going to lose you."

"You're not going to lose me; at least not for a while."

"Not for a long while I hope. Are you going to eat that chicken?"

"No. Sit down. Eat it."

He did so, reaching simultaneously into the deep pocket of his trench coat.

"I didn't know if you would be conscious or not. But I thought if you were, I'd bring you something."

"What is it?"

"It's a copy of my newest novel. Just came out. And a review from *The New York Times*."

"Wonderful. Let's see both of them."

He handed her the hard-backed book, the cover of which was littered with blood covered cadavers.

"Remembering Dismemberment," she read aloud.

"Yeah, it's a little more intellectual than my usual stuff. I wasn't sure if my readers would like it. But this review came out today."

The newspaper page was stuck in the novel. She took it out and looked at it, then read quietly:

This is one of the most disturbing books I have ever read.

"Yeah. Somehow when you get a great review like that it makes all the work worthwhile."

"I can imagine. What else does he say here? *The carnage is incessant and often sickening.*

"Advance sales are through the roof."

"It sounds like a great movie; or better still a television series."

"My agent says he's been approached. But I don't know. I don't trust screenplay writers"

"You think they might miss some of the work's subtlety?"

"I've heard that can happen. Anyway we'll see what their offer is."

"I'll be curious to hear. Does that chicken taste as good as it looks?"

"Sure does. Why didn't you want to eat it?"

"Somehow it didn't appeal to me, not sure why. But now that I've read your review, I think I understand."

"What do you mean?"

"The carnage is incessant and sickening."

"Nina, I'm never sure when you're being serious and when you're joking."

"Me neither. But Tom, really, thank you for coming to see me. And thanks for showing me the book."

"It's a signed copy. I'll leave it with you, if you need something to read tonight."

"Wonderful. It sounds like the perfect book to read in a hospital."

"See there it is again, that sense of humor."

"I'm being perfectly serious. And I promise you, I'll have it read before morning."

"I'll be anxious to hear what you think."

"I'll give you my honest opinion," she lied, knowing that she would neither read the book (She had never read more than a page or so of any of Tom's books, and could not imagine ever doing so in the future) nor tell Tom the truth about her feelings about it. "Now go home though, and begin writing another one. I've got to get quiet and rest. And don't forget: tell whoever is standing out in front of the hospital in the rain…"

"It's sleet now."

"Oh my God. Well, whatever it is, the population of Bay St. Lucy to get inside and out of it, because I'm perfectly okay."

"All right," he said, finishing the last chicken bit and standing up. "I'll tell them. But Nina, I think Penn is going to come by and see you in a few minutes. She had a winter fishing party today and just got back. If anybody down there tries to stop her…"

"I see what you mean. Well, we'll just have to hope for the best."

"All right. Have a good night then."

And, so saying, he left the room.

She perused the cover of the book for a second or so, wondering where in the room she might hide it so as to eliminate completely all possibilities of waking suddenly in the night and catching a glimpse of it.

She leaned over, dropped it on the floor directly beneath her bed, and carefully covered it with one of the napkins from her dinner plate.

"There," she whispered, feeling as though she had just buried a dead animal.

And there, too, were the flowers and the cards.

She wanted to read those cards as intensely as she wanted not to read Tom Broussard's novel.

So, if she could just swing her legs out of the bed…

"Nina! Dearest, oh so sick Nina!"

There, having just appeared in the same dark doorway that had seconds earlier subsumed Tom Broussard, stood Alanna DelaFosse.

"Nina, oh my God, are you alive?"

She was a profusion of colors, of course, as she was always a profusion of colors, and she seemed out of place in the somber entranceway, belonging with the array of blooming flowers directly opposite.

"I'm alive."

"Thank heaven

Alanna made her way across the room like a moveable Arabian Bazaar.

"Are you certain you're all right, dear?"

"I fine. But how did you get into the hospital after visiting hours?"

"Nina, surely you know that such formalities are not going to hinder me when one of my dearest friends might be at death's door!"

"I'm not at death's door. But how did you get in?"

"I showed them the card that identifies me as one of the hospital's board of directors."

"But you're not one of the hospital's board of directors."

"No, but Edie Towler is, and she happened to be attending a poetry reading at the Auberge des Arts when we heard the news. She wanted to come herself, but I begged so hard for her card that she let me have it, with the stipulation that I return as soon as possible and inform the poetry club of your condition. And speaking of that, whatever *is* your condition? We're hearing all kinds of things!"

"Alanna this is Bay St. Lucy. This town is to gossip what heaven is to Methodists."

"What *did* happen?"

"I had a swollen foot."

Alanna de la Fosse looked at her as though she had said: 'I'm pregnant.'

"A swollen foot?"

"Yes."

"And that's all?"

"Well, it was caused by a blood clot."

'I'm pregnant, and the baby is being born.'

"Nina, that's terrifying."

"It's not terrifying."

"But blood clots can be fatal! If they go to your brain, you can have a stroke—or die immediately!"

"This one is apparently only…"

"How is your recovery to be handled?"

"What do you mean?"

"Who will take care of you, Nina, while this clot threatens you?"

"No one is to 'take care of me.' The doctor says I'm just to go home."

"Alone?"

"Well, there's Furl."

"You need to be serious for a moment about this, Nina."

"All right, I'm serious."

"Nina, I've thought this for quite some time now, and I have no choice but to bring it up now."

"Bring what up?"

"How old are you?"

"Seventy."

A shake of the head.

A bit more silence. Then Alanna stood, walked in a tight circle for a time, looked up at the ceiling, then back at Nina, and said quietly:

"You don't need to be living alone. Not in that shack."

Nina was incredulous.

"I love my shack."

"What if you fall down the stairs?"

"I'm not planning to fall down the stairs."

"My dear, no one 'plans' such things. No one 'plans' blood clots. But they happen. And when they do—to you—you have no business being alone."

"Where would I go? You want me to go to a nursing home?"

Alanna sat again, pulled her chair closer to the bed, and said:

"I think you should come and live at the Auberge."

It took some moments for Nina to grasp this. But once she did, she hardly knew how to answer.

"I—I don't—"

"We could make a delicious little apartment for you. There are, in fact, already two small apartments that we use for visiting artists. It would not take a great deal of work to make one of them very livable for Ms. Nina Bannister."

"Alanna, thank you for the invitation to live at Auberge des Arts. It means a lot to me, it really does. But..."

"But it would work so well, dear. You could be a part of so many cultural events that you are forced to miss now, simply due to logistics. And we could—well, look after each other as we grow older."

"Are you proposing to me?"

A laugh in reply.

"In a way I am. I sometimes tire of my de facto role as Maven of Bay St. Lucy's art scene."

"You need a co-maven."

"I suppose I do."

Nina shook her head:

"I don't think so, Alanna. I love my lifestyle too much."

Although, even as she said the words, Nina could remember her depression from earlier in the evening.

Somehow that was gone now, though.

Somehow the last hours had shaken her free from those feelings.

Now she wanted no more than to be home.

The beach beckoned her.

Her own little cat-littered living room beckoned her.

"I'm going to have to say no, Alanna. Although I appreciate the offer more than I can say."

"But your recovery—"

"I'll be fine, I promise you."

A heavy sigh, then Alanna standing

She picked up her purse, and walked to the door.

Once there she turned back toward the room, said—

"Au revoir my dear dear friend."

And she left.

She had not been gone more than half a minute—not even enough time for Nina to resolve yet again to walk over to read the cards on the flowers—when a mammoth bellowing roar echoed from the outer corridor and into the room. The bellowing could have come from some large enraged animal, except that it periodically transformed itself into words, some of which Nina knew, others she was hearing for the first time.

"YOU B—F—S. DON'T YOU *EVER* TRY TO G—
—AT MY—OR BY N—I'LL—YOUR Y—TO YOUR
J—!!"

An instant later, the door burst open and Penelope Royale stormed in.

She crossed the room, took a six pack of beer from one of the pockets of her wet and ponderous yellow trench coat, and set it on the table.

Then she leaned over Nina, bent still lower, kissed Nina's forehead.

And left.

There was a bit more noise as she made her way out of the building, but there were no gun shots fired and no blows landed.

Within a minute all was quiet again.

The door swung open again and ushered in the largest hypodermic needle she had ever seen in her life, followed by the small One-Hundred-and-One Dalmatians patterned scrub wearing Annie, who was holding the hypodermic needle aloft in front of her.

"Hi, Ms. Bannister," she said, "ready for your shot?"

She pulled up Nina's gown and before Nina could respond, plunged the needle into Nina's stomach. Click. And withdrew it and threw it in the trashcan.

"I just spent the day in the pediatric ward, but I told Bridget I wanted to say hi again and she asked me to give you the shot. "That wasn't too bad, was it?" she said chirpily.

"I...I...I...stomach...what...why..."Nina couldn't get the words out. A shot in her STOMACH?

"Oh, don't worry, Ms. Bannister, that is the only one you'll need. Some people have to give themselves the shots in the stomach for weeks afterward, and some diabetics do it all the time. Gotta run! Sleep well and be well." And she backed her way out of the room, while blowing Nina a kiss.

And finally Nina, actually alone, swung her legs off the bed, grasped the metal frame holding the large jar of IV solution, and made her way clanging over to the wall of flowers.

One by one, in the dim light thrown by the television, she read what was written on them:

TO MY FAVORITE TEACHER

And

WE LOVE YOU, NINA

And

GET WELL FAST

And so on and so on—all beautiful, all making her want to cry.

Until, three flower pots before the end of the row, a small card attached to a spray of roses.

And the words, written in pencil:

NINA: THE FIRST MURDER HAS ALREADY BEEN COMMITTED. THERE WILL BE MORE UNTIL YOU MAKE THEM CLEAR MY FATHER'S NAME. THE CORPSE WILL TELL YOU WHO WE ARE.

CHAPTER FOUR: LA VIE EN ROSE

7 o'clock

It was a vase of roses.

How ironic, she thought.

Then she placed the card back where she'd found it, stuck in the thorny branches that extended some six inches above the top of the dark green vase.

She made her way back to bed, the contents of the card still a photograph in her mind. The words, printed in pencil, as though done by a child.

The writer, though, was no child. She thought *'Fifty thousand dollars? Killing people?'*

She got into the bed, careful that the tube extending from the IV container into her arm was still securely taped in place.

Then she found the small telephone receiver-like apparatus that lay on the table beside her and pressed the red button labeled 'nurse call.'

She was relieved to hear Bridget though a metallic rasp covered her voice:

"Yes, Ms. Bannister—are you all right?"

"I'm fine, but something's happened. Can you find Dr. Singh and come with her to my room—and bring Moon Rivard too. "

"Just give me a minute." There was a 'click' on the other end of the line.

She placed the intercom device back on the table and glanced, almost involuntarily, at the wall that had been covered by flowers.

This had to be a joke.

But a joke played by whom?

Years ago, while she was a principal, there would be the occasional nasty anonymous note delivered to her and Frank. This was the curse of running a school, and some difficult decisions had to be made. Some students had to fail courses and others had to be disciplined in one way or another.

But she was not a principal now, nor had she been for some time. She turned her head away from the flower wall and looked out through the window opposite. Darkness outside, sleet spattering on the window panes, glare from the parking lot beneath. Faintly she could hear the wail of a siren somewhere in the direction of downtown, making its way toward the hospital.

Finally there was a knock on the door.

"Yes?"

"Moon here."

"Come in."

He did so, slumping a little as he entered the room, his yellow rain slicker glistening with melting ice articles in the dim light.

He shook his head.

"That Ms. Penelope! I tell you she's a handful. We tell her she can't come up 'cause it's too late but she don't like to hear that one bit. I got a new man working for me, just hired him yesterday. I thought he was going to try to stop her by force and I catch him just in time. Anybody try to put hands on that woman is going to get his neck broke. Well, no matter, they all gone now, that crowd. Maybe you can get some sleep in a hour or so. How is your ankle, Ms. Nina?"

"It's fine."

"Don't hurt none?"

"No."

"We all glad to hear that. Did you want to see me about something?"

"Do you see that vase of roses over there?"

He turned slightly.

"Yes, ma'am. Look like a dozen of them. Pretty things. Guess you got yourself a suitor. You know, Jackson Florist had to open up special tonight after folks found out you was here. He still open I think, people buying flowers and sending them over. They can't get in to see you themselves, but they want to send something. Must make you feel good."

"Would you go over and look at the card sticking there in the rose stems?"

He set off across the room, smiling over his shoulder as he walked, and saying:

"I bet it's a marriage proposal, dozen roses like that."

He approached the vase and took out the card. She waited. Finally, he put the card back where he found it and, saying nothing, pulled a chair beside her bed. The smile was gone now, and his voice seemed to have dropped an octave.

"Who," he said, "brought you that vase?" His voice was quiet.

"No idea. They took me up into one of the labs to run a test on me. While I was up there, they assigned me this room. The flowers were here when I arrived. What do you make of that card, Moon?"

"I don't know what to make of it."

"A prank?"

"Maybe. Not a very funny one though."

Nina asked, "Could there be fingerprints on the vase?"

"Oh yes, ma'am. Probably a thousand. That there vase has been sitting over in Jackson's store for Lord knows how many months now, before somebody done bought it this evening. Probably covered with prints."

"Yes. I guess that's true."

"And if we could pick out the prints of the one who bought it, all we could do is run them through our system. If it's somebody that been picked up before then all right, we got something. But…"

"But whoever wrote this isn't in any system."

"No, ma'am. I suspect not."

"Whoever wrote this is just a prankster."

"Well, Ms. Nina, I have to tell you, I'm just not too sure how to deal with this problem. We can't find out anything from the vase. We can't find out who left the vase."

Nina shifted in her bed and pulled the covers up a bit. "Does the hospital have a security force?"

"Yes ma'am, us. The Bay St. Lucy Police Force. Years ago—for a long time I think it was—they paid for an outside security service. They had round the clock security protection. Cost an arm and a leg. And what did they get for their money? Five fat guys in uniforms, used to walk up and down the hallways every hour or so, making people nervous. Wasn't no crimes done here. Maybe every six months or so somebody would report a case of drugs gone missing. But even then the folks they hired was useless. Never found anything."

"So now?"

"Now we protect the place as a city service. I send a man around every couple hours through the night. He checks the front desk, be sure everything's all right. Sometimes we do a walk through. That's all it is; that's all there needs to be."

"But now, with this note…"

He rose, stiffly, and shook his head, saying with an air of finality:

"Ms. Nina, I don't believe this thing is any more than some kind of a joke. But I'll tell you what I think should happen. You remember I told you I hired a new man yesterday."

"Yes, the one that Penelope almost killed."

"Would have, if he'd touched her. But whoever wrote this note, even if it's Jack the Ripper, ain't as dangerous as Ms. Penelope. So I'm going to send this young man—he just graduated from the University of Mississippi, degree in Criminol Something."

"Criminology?"

"I guess that's it. Whatever it is, they all seem to have to do it these days before they get to be cops. And I promise you, whatever you need to be a good cop, you don't learn in no college. But anyhow he's a nice enough kid, even though he is a little bookwormish for me. Maybe it's the glasses, I don't know. I'm going to tell him about this little card and send him up to your room."

"What's his name?"

"Yancy. Michael Yancy. His folks are from Hattiesburg. Used to know his papa, even though the old man's gone now. Some time since I seen Michael. He was just a little kid the last time. Good people. But like I say, I'm going to send him up and have him look in on you. Also I'm going to tell him to make the rounds of the hospital for a few hours, just so folks will know the law is here. I don't think there'll be anything for him to do except flirt with the nurses—not that he impresses me as the flirting type—but still it can't hurt. And I think you'll like the kid."

"All right, Moon."

"I gotta go now, but Yancy should be here any time."

He left and was replaced in the room a minute later by Officer Yancy, who looked just as described, only more so. The cap of his uniform seemed too big, resting on his ears and almost covering the required police buzz cut. His pale blue uniform hung on him, and the various attachments and accoutrements which were supposed to make him seem more martial and threatening—sidearm, handcuff set, even badge— seemed to make him look like a cheap hardware store whose wares were in disarray.

And—Moon Rivard was right, she decided—the thick black horned rim glasses did not help his image as a man to be feared.

"Ms. Bannister?"

He had made it into the room with no problem, but he seemed too shy to come closer than five feet to Nina, whom he treated as though she were radioactive.

"Officer Yancy. Thank you for coming."

He seemed to do a quick check of an imaginary mental Geiger counter, found the reading to be within a safe range, and thus allowed himself to take two steps closer, clanking a bit as he did so.

Thank God, Nina found herself thinking, that Penelope Royale had not gotten her hands around his throat.

"No problem, ma'am."

"Why don't you call me Nina. I know I'm old, but 'ma'am' just seems to make it official."

To this he replied with a boyish—of course everything he did was boyish—grin.

"All right, Nina. But like I say, it's no problem. Officer Rivard told me about the card, and what it said. He thinks it's just a joke of some kind."

He was interrupted by the entrance of Bridget and Dr. Singh, who said:

"You sent for the two of us: is there a problem?"

"The two of you should probably read this."

He handed them the card. As they were reading it he said, "We thought it might be a prank. It still might be a prank."

On hearing this, Lalima Singh just shook her head: "It might be. When a patient has trouble breathing, it might be indigestion. Might. Might. Or it might be a heart attack coming on. We're doctors and nurses here. We don't get to do "might." If we do, people can die. This note says that someone has already been murdered. All right. Let us look into that."

She pressed a call button. A raspy response from, Nina assumed, the central nurses' station had just begun to trickle out of the phone when she interrupted it, saying quietly but firmly:

"I want you to do a complete check of hospital personnel. Yes, everybody. From doctors down to wall painters. You are to page everybody right now and continue paging until you get an immediate response. I want to know what room they're in and what the hell they're doing. As soon as you've got confirmation on everyone, you call me back. Then, once that's done, send out another message, asking if anyone has seen a suspicious person in the hospital. That should be easy now, since visiting hours are over. Anyone suspicious is not to be approached. We simply need the location reported. We shall take care of it from there. Now get to work. Let me know when you're done."

She flipped off the intercom switch and dropped the speaker into her pocket.

Moon:

"Dr. Singh, how long you think it will take to get all these reports?"

She shook her head. "Ten to twenty minutes. More than half the staff will respond immediately, because that's what they're trained to do. The others though are occupied in something they can't quit. They're giving an MRI or they're taking blood, or they may just be moving a bed from one room to another. At any rate, it's unrealistic to expect everyone in the hospital to respond immediately. But just because some of our people don't call back immediately doesn't mean they've been murdered."

Moon leaned forward in his chair and asked; "All right then. I have to ask you: what do you want me to do?"

"I don't understand your question."

"It's a pretty simple one. We've had a threat and it is scary. But we've had no murder as far as we know of. We've had no violence of any kind. I understand what you said a little while ago about hospital people not being able to take chances—but despite that, I'm in a hard position here."

"I understand that, Officer Rivard."

"I got a few people on my staff. Some of them are off duty now, others on patrol out in the town. Do I call them all back in, bring them over here to the hospital? What do I have the folks do once they get here? Should we make some kind of announcement about this threat? A thing like that may be hard on your nurses and orderlies, but if it gets out—and it will get out, ma'am—it's gonna be even harder on your patients. How many of them you got?"

"Fifty three beds are occupied at the present time."

"You want them worrying that everybody who looks like a nurse or doctor may be someone that…"

He did not finish the sentence, but looked directly at Nina as he started another one:

"And, Ms. Nina, we need to talk about you a little. The question is, why has this card been sent to you? It's as though whoever wrote it trusts you and wants you to know what's happening."

"I'd be flattered if we weren't dealing with murder."

"Right. So what we've got to ask ourselves is…"

Bridget O'Leary's phone buzzed.

"Bridget here."

"Nurse O'Leary, I thought you'd like to know, we just got a call."

"Yes?"

"Accident victim."

"What kind of accident?"

"The caller didn't say, but the call came from Grierson Drive."

"Do they want an ambulance?"

"No, ma'am, they're bringing the victim in by car."

"All right, then, you know the drill. Have Mark and Ted get the stretcher ready, and then be sure we have…"

"Ma'am—"

"Yes, what is it?"

"I just…maybe I shouldn't be taking up your time with this, because, yes, we do know the drill and I know you're in an important meeting and all but I just—well you've not lived in Bay St. Lucy too long so you might not know, and—"

"And what?"

But it was Nina—Nina who had lived in Bay St. Lucy for very long, for her entire life, who said quietly:

"Bridget, there is no Grierson Drive in Bay St. Lucy."

Silence for a time.

Then Michael Yancy said calmly, "I need to go down and meet this car, Moon."

"You better let me do it, son."

A shake of the head.

"You hired me to be a policeman. Well, this may be a job for a policeman. If you're going to look at me all the time like I'm your son…"

Moon nodded, saying, "Yeah, you're right. Hell, an accident happens, folks panic, probably just give the lady the wrong address. But you go on down there, help them meet that car."

"Thanks."

And, so saying, Michael Yancy rose and left the room.

After he was gone, Nina asked:

"You sure that was smart, Moon?"

"Yes. The boy was right. If he wants to be a policeman in this town or any other, he's gonna have to do things a lot harder than meet a car that don't seem to know where it's coming from."

She nodded, was silent for a while, then swung her legs off the table, saying:

"Bridget, help me here."

"What are you doing for God's sakes?"

"I want to go over by the window. It looks down on the main entrance."

"What do you want to do that for?"

"I like that boy."

"Good. I like him too. Now get back in bed."

"No."

"Nina, I order you to get back in bed."

"So what are you going to do, make me?"

"I outweigh you by a hundred and twenty pounds."

"Yes, but I'm wiry. Now come on—push the IV behind me."

"Your ankle is…"

"The least of anybody's worries. Now come on, HOOPSA!"

And so exclaiming, she jumped onto the hard tile floor, which felt cold to her feet. One step across the room—clank, clank—Bridget and the whole IV apparatus following… At the wall of jungle now, parting a few ferns to see?

The circular driveway of the Emergency Entrance. On beyond, the road into town. Streetlights glittering, but no traffic to speak of. A car sat parked against the driveway. Then the door of the ER opened. Michael Yancy took a step toward the car. A second step.

And then the car blew up.

CHAPTER FIVE: ON THE NECESSITY OF STAYING IN THE ROOM

She was first aware of a blinding white flash, as though the sun had detonated beneath her. Then the white gave way to alternate ribbons of yellow and black, as flames and smoke clouds shot upward from what had been the car and lapped against her second floor window.

"Oh no!" came a voice behind her, but it was so close to a scream that she had no idea who uttered it. Nor had she time to turn and look back into the room before an inverted rain storm began, with fragments of metal and glass exploding upwards, pattering on the window and outer walls.

"Nina, get away from the window!"

This had to be Bridget shouting at her because Moon was already hurtling through the door and out into the corridor.

"Get away!"

Somehow she could not. She stood with her nose ball pressed against the glass, which was already growing noticeably warmer, immersed as it was in the convection currents being emitted by the blaze beneath.

"Here! Come on! You've got to come here!"

Bridget's powerful grip was around her arm now, and she could feel herself being pulled backwards toward the bed. But she still did not turn her eyes away from the parking circle below, which was filling with nurses and orderlies, all ringing themselves as close to the fire as was tolerable.

"What happened?" said a voice that sounded strange to her, mixing as it was with the cacophony of screams and shouts and fire-roar and growing wailing sirens that seemed to be springing up from everywhere at once. The voice, she then realized, was hers.

"Come on!" Bridget kept repeating. Though her grip on Nina's arm was tightening, her voice was calm.

"What happened?"

"A car blew up."

"What car? Who..."

"I don't know, honey. But I've got to get down there! Now get into bed!" said Bridget, throwing back the covers.

"Michael! Michael Yancy was down there! I heard him! He was just coming out of the ER!"

"Come on, put your legs up here!"

She did so, and within seconds, she was lying on her back again, looking up at the ceiling but aware of the glow behind the plants on the wall to her right.

Both of Bridget's hands were on her shoulders now, and the woman's face was within a foot of her own.

"Nina! Are you all right?"

"Yes!"

"Can you see? Can you see me? You were looking right down at that thing when it blew! Are you sure your head doesn't hurt?"

"I'm sure. But Michael was down there! He was just going out through the door when it..."

"I know, Nina. Now listen to me! Are you listening?"

"Yes, I'm listening!"

"I've got to go down there right now. Do you understand that?"

"Yes!"

"Are you sure?"

"I'm sure."

"A car just blew up. I don't know why it blew up; I don't know if anybody was in it; I don't know how close anybody was to it when it exploded. But I've got to get down there NOW, do you understand that?"

"Yes, I do," she said. "Yes, I do." But in truth she did not understand it. She did not understand any of it. It was like a bad dream.

"We have to leave you alone here for a few minutes. Are you going to be okay?"

The nightmare continued. Nina, unable to make it stop or wake up, merely nodded, and then said: "We shouldn't have let Michael Yancy go down there by himself! If he's…"

"We don't know if he's even hurt, Nina. I'm going down to find that out. But I need for you to promise me something, okay?" Bridget was edging toward the door of Nina's hospital room. She paused as Nina repeated "Yes."

"You just stay in this room! As soon as I can, I'll send someone up to be with you and tell you what's going on. But right now I have to go. Just promise me, you won't take one step out of this room!"

"All right. I promise."

"Good girl. I'll see you as soon as I can!" So saying, Bridget whirled and ran out of the room.

Count to ten, Nina, she told herself. *One two three four… Stay in the room. Stay in the room. Bridget knows best; Bridget knows best of course, you're got to stay in the room…five six seven eight…*

And no matter what is going on downstairs, no matter what has happened to the young and affable Michael Yancy who resembles in no way a police officer and should never have been sent downstairs to meet a fake call from a street that has never existed in Bay St. Lucy—no matter all or any of these things, Nina, you would only be in the way.

A car blew up. What can you do to help in that situation? As for the roses and the cards, this accident might have nothing to do with them. Cars blow up. Even in hospital parking lots. *Nine ten.*

She could see out into the hallway, where chaos reigned. All of the doors were opened. Patients wandered in and out of rooms, asking each other what had happened, walking a few steps down the corridor, and then flocking into those rooms whose windows offered a view of the driveway.

"What is happening?"

"My God, what's going on down there?"

"Has there been a wreck?"

"It's a terrorist attack, that's what it is!"

"It's ISIS, that's what it is!"

She decided to disobey Bridget. She could not go downstairs nor could she disconnect herself from the IV. But she could make her way back over to the window and from there see what was happening with the fire. And this she did, laboriously, clumsily—but effectively.

Ten steps and she was parting greenery again. The window was hot and she had no wish to open it. But through it she could see clearly.

People, most of them blue-clad with ID lanyards hanging down in front of their chests, were running this way and that, neglecting the sleet and cold, all of them making a circle around the fire, as though they were preparing to roast marshmallows at some ghoulish bonfire. Some of them were talking to or screaming at each other, saying words which Nina, insulated by the thick plate glass, could not hear. Yet more of them were occupied with their own personal smart phones, which she assumed were being used to reassure family members.

She saw a fire truck arrive, its crew leaping to the pavement and madly tearing hoses off their mountings. Soon powerful sprays of water attacked and were instantly subsumed by the blaze, which even from Nina's glassed-in room could be heard bellowing like an angry creature. She thought she could even see parts of the car—a fender? A door?—blackened beyond any type of recognition.

Within two minutes or so, the powerful water sprays began to do their jobs, and the fire started to abate. She saw a van arrive with the call letters WCBN painted across it. Several figures jumped out of it, two carrying cameras and one a microphone.

"Television," she whispered to herself.

She returned to the bed, where she found the remote control device. This red button—on. VCR—no. What about this green button? She pushed it and it worked.

"This is Chip Herndon from WCBN News, Bay St. Lucy. I'm standing in front of Bay St. Lucy Hospital, where just moments ago, a car exploded, actually within fifty feet of the entrance to the Emergency Ward. As you can see, The Bay St. Lucy Fire Department has been summoned, and the blaze resulting from the car's explosion is now almost out. As for injury, cause of fire, and other matters, we're only speculating at this time, but we do have on hand Officer Moon Rivard of the Bay St. Lucy Police Department, who may be able to answer some of our questions. Officer Rivard?"

And there was Moon.

"Officer Rivard, can you tell us if there were any injuries resulting from this explosion?"

"Nobody we know about," said Moon, shifting his weight uneasily from right to left.

"What about the driver?" persisted Herndon, moving closer.

"Driver's seat was empty," answered Moon, taking a step backward. He removed his hat and wiped his hand across his brow and then resettled the hat on his curl-encrusted head.

"Do you know how the car got here?"

"Nope." He shook his head. "It was parked in a 'no parking' area on the entrance circle. But nobody from reception remembers seeing it pull up, or seeing anyone get out of it and walk away."

You have no idea why the car exploded?"

The crowd continued to grow. Some of the people carried umbrellas, unfurled against the sleet. Others huddled together in pairs, their shoulders hunched against the cold. Still more seemed to be ignoring the cold and sleet and pressed closer to Moon and Herndon.

"We don't. The Fire Department's going to be able to tell us more on that, but we've got to give them a little time." Moon glanced back over his shoulder at the crowd.

"Could it have been a car bomb?"

"Could have been lots of things, but I don't want to guess about it now."

"Is there any indication that this might have been a terrorist attack?"

"Nope." He looked behind him, seemingly searching for an escape route. Finding none, he turned back resignedly into the stream of never-ending questions. "Nobody's claimed responsibility for it," he grumbled.

"Is there any more you can tell us at this time, Officer Rivard?"

"No. All I can do is praise the fire department. They got here within a minute or so of the explosion, and they did a great job."

"All right then—thank you, Officer Rivard."

And Moon was gone.

The television returned to its usual banality; the corridor outside began to quiet a bit; and nothing was left for Nina to do but push the red 'off' button and stare for a time at the window, through which she could now see nothing at all.

There was nothing to do but return to bed. And think. 'The first murder has already been committed.' But, according to Moon, no one had been in the car. It made no sense. And what was her role in all of this? Where was Jane Austen when she was needed?

"A mind lively and at ease can do with seeing nothing, and can see nothing that does not answer."

Nina's mind might well have been satisfied with seeing nothing, but her eyes had seen far too much. How could she...

This train of thought was interrupted by the entrance of Bridget O'Leary, and immediately behind her, Dr. Singh. Dr. Singh stepped forward toward Nina's bed.

"How is Michael Yancy?" asked Nina, resisting the urge to get out of bed.

Bridget and Dr. Sing stood by Nina's bed. Dr. Singh answered, "He's fine, Nina. He was just going out the door when the car blew up. The force of the blast knocked him down onto the driveway and he has a cut on his forehead. Otherwise, he's perfectly okay. I was in the room downstairs when he briefed Moon about the whole thing. Apparently when he got downstairs, he looked outside to see if this 'accident car' was in sight. It wasn't. Instead, he saw a brown Ford escort illegally parked on the far side of the circular driveway. It seemed strange to him. He asked at reception, but nobody had seen it pull up. When he went outside to check on it...well, you know."

"Yes, I know."

There was a pause, then Dr. Singh walked to Nina's bed and pulled up a chair. She asked:

"How are you feeling?"

"I'm fine, Dr. Singh."

"Let me see your ankle."

Nina pulled her leg out from under the cover and let Dr. Singh feel her ankle.

"Good. The swelling is down. Explosions and death threats seem to agree with you."

"It's just my nature."

"I understand. There is something, though, that I must ask you."

"All right."

"I wish, of course, for you to stay here in the hospital tonight. We need to keep you on the IV at least for the next few hours, and well into the morning. This would be ideal. But the card was addressed to you, and it seems to threaten that more violence will occur here in the hospital. A certain amount of violence, as we know, has already occurred. Now, I must make this clear to you: a hospital cannot close for inclement weather. There are patients here who cannot leave, and who cannot simply be sent home in a winter storm. And we as professionals must do everything possible to take care of these people."

"I see that."

"But these things do not necessarily apply to you."

"What do you mean?"

"I mean that I have spoken with young Officer Yancy and with his supervisor, Officer Rivard. We agree that, should you wish not to remain here in the hospital tonight, I would be willing to sign a release. Your condition is not that serious in my view. It could easily be arranged to have an officer assigned to guard your house—and you—during the night. Or for as long as is deemed necessary. What I'm saying to you, Nina, is that if you wish to go home, where you might feel safer, that is certainly possible."

Nina thought about this for a time and was about to answer, when Frank walked into the room and sat down beside her.

Hi, haven't talked with you for a while.

No, Frank, you haven't. Where've you been?

Heaven.

Everything okay up there?

About normal. By the way, it's not really 'up,' you know.

I thought we agreed not to go into that metaphysical stuff.

You're right. Sorry.

So what should I do here?

He imaginary smiled:

Is there any question?

Well, there's a little bit of a question. I mean, there's a killer loose here; he's threatening to kill a lot of people and says he's already killed one. We don't know. The killer might be a member of the hospital staff or someone outside.

You forgot another possibility.

Yeah, what's that?

It could be a patient.

You may be dead but you're not dumb.

I'm just saying…

So the truth is, it could be anyone. And common sense might say, Nina get the hell away from there!

We don't like to use that word 'hell' too much.

Sorry. But you see what I'm saying.

Sure but you're not going anywhere. You know that. You know it without even having me here to tell you.

And why am I not going anywhere?

Because this is Bay St. Lucy, Nina. This is *your* Bay St. Lucy. You're not going to desert the hospital, you've not going to desert the community—and you're not going to desert your people. Good bye.

And not really saying these or any words, he disappeared.

"I'm staying," she said.

Lalima Singh smiled. "I'm glad. I'm truly glad."

As Dr. Singh and Bridget were leaving, they were met at the door by Michael Yancy with Moon Rivard following close behind.

Nina sat up in the bed with a big smile on her face. "Michael, how are you?"

He formed a near smile.

"Funny Ms.—sorry, Nina—but it's funny. You're up here with a blood clot and you're asking me how I am."

"That's right, I am. How are you?"

"Little shaken. I never saw a car blow up before."

"Well, you haven't lived in Bay St. Lucy," said Nina. Moon Rivard chuckled.

"No, ma'am. It's all new to me. But I'm fine. Little scrape on the forehead."

"I asked him," interjected Moon, "if he thought this was a good time to be giving out parking tickets."

Michael shook his bandaged head:

"It's just—there was something not right about it being parked there."

"It's a scary thing," said Nina. "But the good thing is, nobody was hurt."

Silence for a time.

"Sit down, Officer Yancy," said Moon.

Both of the men took chairs. There was a kind of silence that should not have existed, a toxic silence that spread through the air of the room like noxious gas. A mind lively and at ease can do with seeing nothing. But not for long.

"What is it, Moon?"

He bent his head and seemed to speak to the floor.

"We didn't think there was nobody hurt. That's what I told the T.V. man."

"I know. I saw the broadcast."

"But when I talked to him, well, the fire was just being put out. They hadn't been able to get inside the car and look around. Too hot, still smoking."

"All right. Go on."

Although she seemed to know what was coming.

"When they did…" Moon paused and grimaced. He continued but did not look up from the floor.

"Finally, they did get in and could check what had been the back seat."

Nina's palms involuntarily covered her face, and her voice seeped through them.

"Go ahead. Tell me."

"They found a body."

"Whose body?" Nina cried.

"No way to know. Fingerprints burned off. Just…everything all burned up."

"So there's no way to know if whoever was back there had been murdered."

"Yes, ma'am. There's a pretty good way to know."

He reached into his pocket and produced a black and twisted length of metal.

"What is that?"

"'These were handcuffs. Whoever it was had been handcuffed to the door handle in the back seat."

"So the victim was alive when the car blew up?"

Moon shook his head:

"Don't think so. If he had been, Yancy here would have seen him. More likely he'd been killed earlier and put in the back of the car."

"So why the handcuffs?"

"To hold him in place so the explosion wouldn't blow him out of the car. Whoever did this wanted us to find the body right there—and with this little metal locket chained tight to the cuffs."

"What is that thing?"

"Like I say, Nina, it's a locket. We opened it. This little slip of paper was in it. Here."

He stretched out his arm and handed her a small white slip of paper.

She took it and read its message aloud:

"NINA: DON'T FORGET FRANCINE, CORY, AND HARRISON MORGAN."

Silence for a time. "Do you remember these people, Nina?" asked Yancy.

And she could only nod, saying quietly:

"Oh yes. Yes I do."

Then:

"Yes I do. And so does Moon. And I think we need to call Jackson Bennet."

CHAPTER SIX: THE CORY STORY

Fourteen years earlier, Nina recalled.

The hospital was only a few years old then. Frank was an established attorney. Nina had been principal for several years and had settled into the job as well as would ever be possible. The high school, living in the timeless world of all high schools, was just the same as today and just the same as fifty years ago: students jostling each other in the halls, football players happily elbowing one another and careening into the metal lockers, which rattled and groaned under the force of the blows.

"Ms. Bannister?"

She could still remember the voice, still remember turning as, while avoiding simultaneously a fullback, a middle linebacker, and a cheerleader, she turned to address a young woman—Francine Morgan—who taught, just as she herself had taught years earlier, English and American literature.

"Ms. Bannister?"

"Yes, Francine?"

Francine Morgan.

Blue-blonde, blue-blonde. Strange what one remembers after all the years. Francine standing there before her in the main corridor, wearing a cornflower blue dress. Short-haired, but so blonde. Blue dress and oh so blonde blonde blonde hair.

"Can I talk to you for a minute?"

A much harder question than it seemed, because, in the life of a really good principal, which Nina was and always had been, there are no free minutes. A thousand dramas are always getting ready to be played out, a few of them inspiring, the vast majority of them very bad and very much to be prevented.

"Sure. Come into the office."

Normally she would have suggested the small snack bar which served as a surrogate office but gave a better view of the hallways and classrooms. But something about this did not seem normal.

And so within a few minutes, she found herself looking half at Frank's picture, which sat on her mahogany desk, and half at cornflower blue dressed and innocent as the day is long Francine, who was biting her lip and gripping re-gripping re-re-gripping her hands, looking ever so much like a sophomore who had just learned she was pregnant.

"I'm sorry to bother you like this. I know you're busy."

"That's all right, Francine."

"I have fourth period free so I'm not missing class."

"I know."

And, of course, Nina did know. Along with thousands of other details.

"So what is it, Francine?"

"It's Harrison."

Her husband.

What in heaven's name could Nina do for Harrison?

"Is he ill?"

A shake of the head.

"No. No, his health is fine."

"Then…"

"Ms. Bannister, I've just learned about this. He told me last night."

Another woman, Nina could remember thinking. Of course another woman. And now he's leaving you.

Leaving you and your thirteen year old son—what was
the boy's name?

Ah yes.

Cory.

So is it another woman? she almost asked.

But didn't.

Good thing, because it wasn't.

"Ms. Bannister, Harrison has been accused of a
crime."

"What crime, Francine?"

Adultery. Another woman.

"Embezzlement."

Whoooah!

Another woman would have been so much easier.

"That can't be!"

"I know it can't be; but it is. They're accusing him
of taking fifty thousand dollars."

"But that's absurd, that's…"

"A nightmare. But we're living it."

"What makes them believe this?"

Francine shook her head.

"You probably know he's an administrator at Bay
St. Lucy Hospital."

"Yes. In fact I think I heard Frank say a few weeks
ago that he had gotten a promotion. Frank is much more
aware of the goings on around town than I am."

"He was made Chief Financial Officer."

"Quite an honor."

"It was an honor. And I was so proud. But yesterday
there was a surprise audit of the books. The money
simply wasn't there. The auditors say the only
possibility is that Harrison simply took it. Nina, they're
threatening to have him arrested!"

"What can I do to help, Francine?"

"Your husband is an attorney. The word is that he's
the town's best."

"I'm not sure that's true. But Frank works hard, and he has had some successful cases."

"Would he consent to represent Harrison?"

"I don't know. I can certainly ask him."

"We can't pay hundreds of thousands of dollars. We're not a big corporation."

"Francine, Frank doesn't do work for big corporations. Mostly his clients are people just like you and Harrison. I'm sure that something can be worked out."

So that evening she told Frank of the matter. The two of them were dining at Sergio's by the Sea, a new restaurant in town that had become notable for two things: an exquisite sea bass dinner and a location near the center of town, nowhere near the sea.

She was having the bass, and, she now remembered, an excellent red wine.

"I may have gotten a client for you today, Frank."

"Oh? And how did you do that?"

"One of the teachers, Francine Morgan, asked to see me. It seems her husband—I don't know if I should even be telling you this. It concerns Harrison Morgan, but it sounds very confidential."

He was eating oysters on the half shell. He let a particularly large one slide down his throat and said:

"You don't have to tell me; I already know. Harrison Morgan is the Chief Financial Officer for Bay St. Lucy Hospital. He tried to embezzle fifty thousand dollars. If the hospital doesn't get it back immediately, they're going to prosecute. He can go to jail for a long time."

She can remember looking at him with astonishment, as she often did in those days.

"How did you know that?"

And his Frank-like shrug:

"Everybody in town knows it."

"How does everybody in town know it?"

"This is Bay St. Lucy. Anyway he called me late this afternoon. He's coming to see me tomorrow morning."

"Are you going to take the case?"

"Probably."

"Can you help him?"

"Can I have a bite of that sea bass?"

"Sure. Here."

"Mmm. Good. Want an oyster?"

"No, they're slimy things. Can you help him?"

"Maybe. I know a couple of the board members. They're all old money. Some have partnered with Homer Baron Robinson and he's helped them all get rich. They're not kind men, and they look at people like the Morgans as intruders in the city's aristocracy. A lot of them don't think he should ever have been given the promotion he got. But if, privately, I can convince them to hold off prosecuting him, and he's willing to give the money back, they may be satisfied with just firing him and avoiding the terrible publicity something like this always brings with it.

Except, of course, it did not work out that way.

Harrison Morgan insisted that he did not have the money, and had no idea where it had gone.

He thus was forced to go to trial with no real defense at all, since the auditors testified that he must have it.

Francine Morgen went personally to each of the hospital directors and begged them to show some leniency, pleading his innocence. She was so desperate she went repeatedly to the hospital to plead with any doctor or nurse until that day everyone had had enough and she was escorted from the building.

Everyone was unyielding.

Fifty thousand dollars is fifty thousand dollars.

He was convicted and sentenced to go to prison for fifteen years.

He was to be incarcerated in Hattiesburg.

A special car was to come to his home at ten o'clock on the morning of January 15 to take him away.

Except that the night before the car was to come, he had hung himself.

The body was discovered by their thirteen-year-old son, Cory, who called the police to report the death. As soon as his body had been buried, Francine and Cory left Bay St. Lucy. They said, "Good-bye," to no one and no one in Bay St. Lucy ever saw nor heard from either of them again. And the fifty thousand dollars was never found.

Jackson Bennet arrived at the hospital at 6:15 and was ushered immediately up to Nina's room. Michael Yancy was making the rounds of the hospital corridors. Lalima Singh was seeing patients, but Bridget was there as was Moon.

"Jackson, thank you for coming."

Jackson sat in one of the chairs and scooted it closer to Nina's bed. "Of course, Nina. How are you?"

"My ankle is fine. Otherwise, I've been better."

"I understand. Moon, it's been a tough day I guess."

Moon Rivard smiled weakly:

"Not one of our real good ones."

"You told me on the phone there was a body in the car?"

"There was."

"Still haven't identified it?"

"Nope. Not much to go on. It's at the morgue."

"And you asked me to find out all I could about Cory Morgan."

"That's right."

"Why, may I ask?"

Moon showed him the slip of paper and said, quietly:

"I didn't much want to talk about this on the phone."

Jackson read the note and whispered:

"My God."

"So you see why we need to know about this boy."

"Yes. Of course I do."

Frank's old law partner, leaned back in the chair, his athlete's body straining the metal.

"All right. You probably remember the boy's father killed himself after being convicted of embezzling fifty thousand dollars.

Nina pushed the button and raised herself up a little before saying, "But after the suicide, Jackson—I remember Frank and you—you had just started working at the firm—I remember the two of you working to find the money and clear his name and get Cory and his mama back."

"We did. The family's funds were frozen, but Frank kept looking for the embezzled money. He thought it would go a long way toward easing public opinion of the Morgan family and help Cory and his mother return."

"For how long, Jackson?"

"Frank looked almost every day for at least a year. The practice suffered a bit as he let other work slide. Finally, he had to stop looking…"

"I remember that time, Jackson. He would work late and sometimes even go over to New Orleans following clues. I was worried about him, but after he stopped looking, things went back to normal."

Jackson shook his head. "I was worried about him, too, I have to admit. But he never found the money so we assumed it was taken by Ms. Morgan to get her started in a new life with her son. Once Frank realized they probably had the money, his heart went out of finding it for them. But if Cory, or someone who knows the story, is here, and has killed someone, I guess we still don't know what happened to the money."

"So what," Moon asked, "do we do now?"

"Well, we don't know where Cory Morgan has been for the last ten years. But apparently he's here now. The question is, how do we protect ourselves from him?"

Silence for a time in the room.

"I don't understand," said Nina. "The notes seem to say that everyone in the hospital is in danger. But it was the board alone that made the decision to prosecute Harrison Morgan. Why doesn't Cory just go after them, at least those who are still living?"

"Nina, when this boy saw his father dangling there by a rope, he clearly had very limited understanding of what was going on. He certainly didn't understand what a 'Board of Directors' was. He did know that his dad worked at the hospital, and that now the hospital was destroying all their lives. That's what he may have been thinking of for all these years."

"But why has he waited all these years to get his— well, I suppose we would have to say his vengeance?"

"That I don't know. It certainly doesn't seem to make sense. But I guess I have to tell you this, although it's hard.

"Go ahead," said Moon.

"All right. We might as well all know what we're dealing with here. Some years ago I was part of a team of lawyers that defended a serial killer. The murders were done in Jackson. I interviewed a psychiatrist, who told me that the defendant had almost certainly undergone a break with reality, sometimes believing that he was compelled to murder by entities such as the Devil or God. The two most common groups of people who believe this way are "demon mandated" and "God mandated.""

"You think Cory believes that God wants him to do this?"

"God or the devil. Hardly matters which. He feels that the hospital itself, and all the people in it, have committed a terrible sin, and it's his job to punish them."

"There's another label for people who feel this way, isn't there, Jackson?"

"Yes. didn't want to say it."

"Go ahead."

"All right. Cory may be a psychotic killer. And he's stalking everyone connected with this institution, from the doctors to the nurses to the patients."

More silence.

Finally, Moon:

"What do we do? I've read up some on these kinds of people, though I never yet had to deal with one."

"Until now."

"Yeah. Until now. But as I remember, they can be damned clever."

"Yes, that's my understanding also. They're homicidal and they're insane; but they're not stupid."

"So we can't assume that he's going to make a lot of mistakes and give himself away."

"No, the truth is, we can be pretty sure he won't do such things."

"I still don't understand," said Nina, "why he might have sent those cards to me."

Jackson stood, took several paces in a tight circle, then looked down at her:

"I've been thinking about that myself, Nina. What it seems to me is, during those terrible times, when Frank was defending Harrison, did you go over to the Morgan's house?"

She nodded:

"Yes. I would take dinner over there from time to time and be a shoulder for Francine to cry on."

"That's probably it. He still thinks of you as someone he can trust. He's using you as his messenger, just as God used the prophets."

"How did he know I was even in the hospital?"

Jackson shook his head and almost laughed:

"Nina, the whole Gulf Coast knows you're in the hospital, and has since you checked in. If he was in town he had to hear it."

"Well," said Moon, "at least Nina may be safe. As for the rest of the story though, I just tell you. It's getting late and there's a damned sleet storm going on outside. There's more than two hundred people in here, doctors, nurses, interns, aids, patients, relatives—and every one of them threatened by a psychotic killer that we can't even get a picture of. I don't much see how the situation could be any worse."

At that moment, Lalima Singh walked into the room and said:

"A journalist whose name is Herndon just entered the hospital. He seems quite angry. He is demanding an interview with Ms. Bannister, which I, of course, denied. I told him to stay downstairs in the reception area, that this was a hospital and not an amusement park. I asked Officer Yancy to keep him where he was. He says though that he has just received certain information which concerns the safety of everyone in the hospital."

"Well," said Moon, "at least we know he's downstairs and can't come up here. It's also sure he can't know about the body. And he certainly can't know about Cory Morgan."

At that moment, Chip Herndon burst red-faced into the room, with an obviously embarrassed Michael Yancy a step or two behind him, and said:

"I know about the body, and I know about Cory Morgan."

"I guess we see now," said Nina, quietly, "how the situation could be worse."

CHAPTER SEVEN: THE POWER OF THE PRESS

"I had attempted," said Dr. Singh, stepping to the middle of the room, "to make it clear, Mr. Herndon, that you were not to come up here. I had also asked Mr. Yancy to make certain you did not do so."

"I'm sorry," said Yancy. "I just couldn't…"

"He couldn't stop me. What did you want the boy to do, shoot me? With two photographers looking on?"

"All right Herndon," said Moon, grudgingly. "You're here and we're not going to shoot you. I hope you realize though that Ms. Bannister is a patient in this hospital."

Chip Herndon nodded at Nina.

"Ms. Bannister, I'm genuinely sorry to bother you. I'm a great fan of yours. You may remember you were gracious enough to let me do a story on you and the Lissie movement."

"It's all right, Mr. Herndon. I'm not in any pain, and I was thinking just a few hours ago how lonely I was going to be tonight. Hasn't worked out that way. We might even offer you a glass of good red wine. My friends gave me some when I checked in. It's being held hostage downstairs."

"Ha. I remember now your sense of humor."

"Actually, I'm not using it right now. We really do have…oh well, let that go."

"I'll try not to take too much of your time, and I've left the photographers downstairs. But there is certain information that I've received…"

"What is," Moon interrupted, "this information?"

But Chip Herndon continued to interrogate Nina:

"I received a call about fifteen minutes ago. The caller said that a body had been found in the car that exploded tonight. He also said that you had received a death threat to hospital personnel. Finally, he asked me to ask you about Cory Morgan—actually to get you to 'tell the story' of Cory Morgan to the town. So I am asking you right now: who, Ms. Bannister, is Cory Morgan?"

"Don't answer that, Nina," said Moon.

Herndon whirled and confronted him:

"What are you doing? She has to answer that!"

"The hell she does!"

"Or *you* do! I don't care which it is. But the people have a right to know this information!"

"Yeah, well I've got a right to know something too."

"What?"

"Who made that call?"

"I'm not at liberty to say. My sources are confidential."

"So the newspaper can keep secrets but the police can't?"

The reporter was silent for a time; then his tone seemed to soften.

"Look, Moon, we've worked together before."

"Yeah, we have."

"You understand my situation and I understand yours. In an ongoing police investigation there are certain facts you can divulge and certain ones you have to keep confidential. But if the citizens of Bay St. Lucy—any citizens—are in danger, they have a right to know what's going on. So okay, maybe we trade bits of info, all right?"

"Go on."

"As for the call, I'm not stonewalling you on it. It did come in on my smartphone about fifteen minutes ago. The caller was anonymous."

"There had to be a number flash up on the screen of that phone."

"There was, and I'm having one of the photo guys check it out now. Whenever he finds out where the call came from, I'll tell you. Now come on: give me something in return."

"All right. There was a card delivered to Ms. Bannister's room. It did make certain threats."

"What did it say exactly?"

"That's all the detail I'm going to go into about the card."

"And the body?"

Moon nodded.

"When you interviewed me that first time downstairs, the fire wasn't really out. Took a while for the firemen to check out the whole car. When they did, they found a body in the back seat."

"Whose body, Moon?"

"We don't know. Burned too bad. Also don't know how the man—if it was a man—died. May have been dead before the explosion, we just don't know."

"Where is the body now?"

"Morgue. I just heard: they gonna do an autopsy tomorrow morning. And I'll match your deal with one of my own: when we find out the identity—if we do— I'll let you know."

"All right, I guess that's all I can expect for right now. You do understand that the things you've just told me, the threats and all info about the body, I going to go live with all that. Got a "Breaking News" radiocast in ten minutes, at ten o'clock."

"Do you have to bring in Ms. Bannister?"

"My caller said she received the card."

"Yeah, and she did receive it. But if you report that, half of Bay St. Lucy is going to show up here with shotguns to protect her."

Herndon nodded:

"All right. We'll keep that quiet for now."

"Thanks. And please, don't say nothing about Cory Morgan. That name is part of the investigation, but it's too early to know exactly which part. We're just guessing. Anything you said about Cory Morgan wouldn't be news; it would be gossip."

A hesitation, then a nod.

"That's a deal."

"One more thing: tell the audience not to panic. We've got police here now. I've just got word that six more guys are being sent over from neighboring towns. The entrance is guarded and there are cops in all the corridors. If this guy as much as shows his face, he's caught."

"All right, you've got it. Now, I've got a broadcast to do."

And he was gone.

After a time, Nina asked:

"Why didn't you tell him about Cory?"

"Because we don't really know anything about Cory. An old sad story that maybe some folks remember and others don't. If I tell that Herndon the Cory Morgan story, the morning papers will all be leading with "Psychotic Killer Escapes, Vows Revenge in Bay St. Lucy.""

"Yes, but maybe that's…"

She was interrupted by Chip Herndon's return:

"Sorry to interrupt Moon. I found out something you're not going to like."

"What's that?"

"The anonymous call I got?"

"Yeah?"

"It came from inside the hospital."

CHAPTER EIGHT: SIXTH PERIOD IN THE AUDITORIUM

8 o'clock

It was Lalima Singh who spoke first:

"Officer Rivard, nothing similar to this has ever happened to me. What should I do? What should all of us do?"

"I don't know exactly. Trying to think. Herndon's gonna make that broadcast in ten minutes. Everybody in town who doesn't hear it will sure as hell hear about it. Patients will be wanting to leave. Relatives will show up here trying to get their loved ones out. You gotta tell me, Dr. Singh, what does this mean medicine wise?"

"It puts the hospital and the patients in a very difficult position. I am the only full time MD on call here at the moment. But there are seven other doctors in Bay St. Louis proper, and four more from neighboring towns, whose patients are here at this time. Some of the patients are in intensive care, and quite simply cannot be moved. Others are elderly and weak. To take them outside at this time of night and in this weather…"

Jackson Bennet cleared his throat and interrupted:

"You might also explain about the insurance situation, Dr. Singh."

"Yes. Any patient may leave the hospital at any time. But doing so without a physician's signed permission absolves the insurance company involved of any responsibility."

"In other words, most of these people who leave will be hit with huge hospital bills."

"Unless their personal physicians sign waivers."

"Can these doctors be reached?"

"Yes. I of course have their numbers."

"Then I would say that one thing to do is call them and apprise them of the situation."

"All right, I shall. But you must understand the dilemma they will find themselves in. It is the same dilemma I find myself in. They are called in the middle of a terrible night and told that, because a sick young boy has made threats and perhaps managed to hide himself somewhere in the building, they must sign a document saying what most of them do not believe, that is, that it is quite all right for a patient under their care to be taken away from Bay St. Lucy Hospital. And there are more legal matters to speak of, Mr. Bennet, and I am sure you know precisely what they are."

"Yes, I think I do."

"Then do you wish to vocalize them or shall I?"

"No, I'll have a go at it. If the hospital allows these people to go out in the middle of the night because it is incapable of providing them security, and even one person suffers personal injury after leaving—a bad reaction to being taken off medication or God forbid a stroke—then there are going to be lawsuits like you wouldn't believe. That kind of scenario could spell the end of the hospital."

Silence for a time. Then Jackson continued:

"This is not like a school. If there is a shooter in the area, the school can simply close down, and it's usually not that difficult for parents to come and pick up their kids. But this? This is a whole different ball game. In this case we have to consider…"

Nina interrupted:

"Jackson, I think it's about ten o'clock. I'm going to turn on the television."

"All right. We might as well hear what the whole town's going to hear."

Nina pushed the green button on the remote device, and immediately Chip Herndon, or at least his image, was in the room with them.

"This is Chip Herndon with WBN News, giving you a fresh account of what seems to be an ongoing story. Some time ago this reporter told you of, and showed you pictures of, a car fire in front of Bay St. Lucy Hospital. At that time, WBN interviewed Officer Moon Rivard, who stated that as far as he knew the car was empty. Now we know that is not true. A body was in fact found in the back seat of the car. No identification of this body has as yet been made, nor do we know for certain whether the victim died in the explosion or was killed first and then placed in the car. Going on: WBN has learned, and has verified, that a threatening message has been received by Bay St. Lucy Hospital. This threat seems to be aimed at any or all hospital personnel. We cannot at this time ascertain the precise nature of the threat. We do know that Bay St. Lucy police are taking the matter very seriously, and that security at the hospital has been stepped up. Officers are here guarding the entrance and patrolling the hallways even as I speak to you. Officer Rivard has asked me to convey to all of you, especially those who might have friends or loved ones being treated in the hospital at the present time, that security here is tight, and that the entire area is well guarded. So, that's all we can tell you at the present, but we will keep monitoring the situation, and we will update you as soon as we know more."

The image disappeared and was replaced by that of a late night talk show host, whom Nina dispatched immediately with a bit of pressure on the red 'off' button.

There was a buzzing sound from the telephone in Lalima Singh's hospital gown pocket.

She took the phone out and flipped it open.

"Dr. Singh."

She listened for a time, remaining motionless as she did so.

Then:

"All right. Just do as you have been doing. I shall be down momentarily."

She flipped the phone shut.

"What is it?" asked Nina.

"The telephones at the reception desk began ringing as soon as Mr. Herndon's broadcast ended. All of the callers are quite concerned, some of them are angry. They want to know precisely what the threat stated, if there is a connection between the threat and the body found in the car, and how dangerous the situation actually is. Some have stated they are coming immediately to the hospital, either to remove their loved ones or guard them personally."

"What are you going to do?"

"I think it prudent now, Officer Rivard, that you and I both go downstairs. Mr. Bennet, you are I take it a well-known and highly respected attorney. Your presence might also help to reassure people."

"Certainly."

"Officer Yancy?"

"Yes, Doctor?"

"It would probably be a good idea for you to remain here with Nina. Given the nature of the situation, I do not believe she should be left here alone."

"I got it."

"All right then. Officer Rivard, Mr. Bennet—let us prepare to receive our visitors."

The three of them left.

Nina spoke to Yancy, who was still standing by the door and peering out into the corridor:

"You might as well sit down, Michael. You're probably going to have a long night in front of you."

He smiled, walked to a chair beside the bed, and sat down.

"This isn't," said Nina, "exactly what you expected when you joined the Bay St. Lucy police force."

"No. Not exactly."

"But I'm curious to know: why do you want to join *any* police force? If it isn't this, it's something just as dangerous. Every time you go in to work, you're risking your life."

"Well, it's not quite that bad. A lot of the job is routine. And as for the rest, I can't imagine doing anything else. My dad was a cop. I idolized him. He even worked with Officer Rivard on a case some years ago. I was just six, but even then I knew. And I loved studying criminology. Found it fascinating. Still do."

"Doesn't your mother worry about you?"

"No. She got used to being the wife of a policeman. Being the mother of one, she always tells me, isn't that different."

"Of course if *you* ever marry—"

"That's not in the cards right now. If anything, I'm married to my work. I really think that in some years I might…"

He was interrupted by a nurse, who stuck her head in the door and said:

"Ms. Bannister?"

"Yes, Judy?"

"We're all watching T.V. at the second floor nurses' station. Some of the other nurses said you might want to see what's going on downstairs. It's pretty bad."

"All right. Thank you."

She left.

"Well, Michael," she said as she pushed the green button, "let's see the worst."

The worst was a wide-angle camera shot of the entire downstairs reception area, which was rapidly filling up with people. The scene was live on the screen, and confused voices could be heard.

"What exactly is happening here?"

"Why didn't you tell the town as soon as these threats were made?"

"What exactly is the police force doing to ensure the safety of people in the hospital?"

And finally, from a woman with a more shrill voice than any of the others:

"Is this an active shooter situation? And if it is, why hasn't the hospital been closed?"

Then she could see that Jackson, Moon, and Lalima Singh were attempting to answer the questions.

Attempting and failing.

They were simply engulfed by the crowd.

"All right," she said quietly.

And got out of bed.

"What are you doing?" asked Michael.

She did not answer.

With her right hand she carefully pulled the IV tube out of her left arm, watched for a time to be sure there was no bleeding from the small puncture where the needle had been—there was none—then let the IV tube dangle in mid-air while she swung her legs out of the bed and let her feet experience yet one more time the cold tile floor.

She walked quickly to the closet in which her clothes had been left, pulled a sweater over her hospital gown, did the same with the pair of dungarees she had been wearing when she came in, pulled a pair of white gym socks over her still swollen foot and her still normal foot, managed to get her tennis shoes on by dint of not tying the left one, and headed out into the hall.

She had the impression that Michael was following her, but she wasn't sure.

She simply walked as briskly as possible down the corridor, which was almost deserted now. People were either in their rooms watching television screens, or they were too scared of 'active shooter' to come out.

She reached the elevator, pressed the button, and waited.

No response.

"Damn," she whispered.

She decided to take the stairs.

Faded green paint bannisters, gray unforgiving steps, low ceiling, stairwell walls beige and rat-maze like…

First floor.

The ankle doesn't hurt, the ankle doesn't hurt…

She pushed open the doors and strode out into the main lobby of the reception area.

Then she turned, transformed herself into Principal Bannister, and said in the not shouting but impossible not to hear voice that principals either develop or die.

"IT IS SIXTH PERIOD AND HERE WE ARE IN THE AUDITORIUM! I WANT YOU ALL TO TAKE YOUR SEATS!"

It worked.

The crowd quietened and looked up at her. A few people actually laughed. Probably because there were no seats to be taken. Of course this was no auditorium, either. But in another way, they were all in school again, and this was their leader.

From somewhere in the audience:

"How are you, Ms. Bannister?" said a young, balding man with a cap meant to cover a bald spot. She recognized the speaker. Of course she recognized most of the people out there.

"I'm fine, Jimmy," she answered to Jimmy Robinson. "I'm fine, all of you. I appreciate your concern. My room is full of flowers."

More laughter.

Then another voice, this one a female, her three-inch heels making her taller than Jimmy Robinson:

"Nina, what's going on? Why won't anybody tell us anything?"

Elaine Barksdale. Cheerleader both her junior and senior year. Dumb as a post.

"There is a situation here, Elaine. And I'm not going to try to make light of it."

"Is there an active shooter in this building? Is this Columbine in a hospital? Because if it is…"

"No, it isn't."

All right, Nina, think.

Why isn't it?

There is a psychotic killer loose in the Bay St. Lucy Hospital.

So why isn't it like Columbine?

"No shots have been fired here."

Good!

Well done, Nina!

So now what do you tell them?

"A threatening note was delivered to my room."

Two steps forward by Billy:

"Ms. Bannister, my mother is in this hospital recovering from a heart attack she had yesterday. Now how am I supposed to leave her here with all of this going on?"

All right. It's time to be Principal Bannister, and explain school policy to the children.

"Billy, you have to leave her here."

"The hell I do. Sorry Ms. Bannister for talking like that. But the hell I do."

"Then what are you going to do with her? It's ten o'clock at night and there's a sleet storm. Who is your mother's doctor?"

"Dr. Hughes from over in Griffithsport. That's where Mama lives now."

"Have you talked to him about this?"

"No, ma'am."

"How old is your mother?"

"She's eighty-two."

"Do you think Dr. Hughes would recommend taking an eighty-two year old heart attack victim out into a sleet storm in the middle of the night—taking her home where there are no medical facilities? You actually feel that he would recommend that?"

"No, ma'am, but…"

"But let's be brutally frank here. Does your mother have insurance?"

"Yes, Ms. Bannister."

Nina shook her head.

"No, she does not. Not if she leaves this hospital without her doctor's signed permission. And Attorney Bennet, who is here with us, assures me that is true in every case."

Another voice, this one from a far corner, and coming from a speaker Nina could not identify.

"If something like this were to happen at a school, they would close the school until they had caught the shooter."

"Yes, but this is not a school. The people in these rooms are not elementary school students nor are they sixteen year olds. They are, at least many of them, eighty-two year olds and they are ill. They are ill or they would not be here."

Silence for a time.

Then Nina continued:

"Listen to me, every one of you. Officer Rivard has policemen all over this hospital. They are guarding all the entranceways and all of the exits. They are patrolling the corridors. They will protect your mother. And they will protect me."

"Ms. Bannister?"

"Yes?"

"I'm Tom Edgarton. I was a senior during your last year as principal."

"I remember you, Tom. Of course I do. The eighty five yard run against Gulfport. No one in Bay St. Lucy will forget that any time soon."

"Thank you, Ms. Bannister. The thing is—well, my wife is a nurse here."

"You married Judy Armstrong."

"Yes."

"I didn't know she worked here."

"She came on shift an hour ago. If I'd known what was going on, I might have told her to stay home."

"And would she have stayed home, Tom?"

Silence for a time, then a shake of Tom's head:

"No, ma'am."

General laughter in the crowd.

"No, ma'am. She takes her job real serious."

"Of course she does. Or she wouldn't be doing this job at all."

"All right, I understand that. I understand that a lot of the patients are real sick, and we depend on the doctors and nurses to take care of them. But I've brought a Smith and Wesson 38 with me. I know how to use it, and so does Judy. It says in the Constitution she has a right to protect herself."

"No, it says she has the right to belong to a well-regulated militia. But it does say in the by-laws of the Bay St. Lucy Hospital that there are to be no weapons of any kind within these walls."

"Tell that to the shooter."

"I'm certain, Billy, that will be one of the first points that Officer Rivard discusses with the person. But I will point out to you: there has been as yet no shooting that we know of."

The crowd had grown silent.

She stepped toward them:

"All of you, think hard about this. The school is important to us, and it's where all of us learn. But the hospital is the heart of any community. We cannot desert or abandon it. If we should do that, then this criminal—I don't know what else to call him or her—would have won. The note said people would die. Well, that would be true, except they wouldn't die at the hand of some wretched killer; they would die because their own community deserted them and ran helter skelter away from their bedside. And why? Because somebody was sick enough to murder somebody else and blow up a car. Is one sick idiot enough to make your abandon your hospital, the place—the sacred place, I've always thought—where your loved ones are cared for, where your children are born, where your elderly are comforted?"

Silence for a time. Then Janet Eisner—honor roll student from twelve years past—stepped forward and asked:

"All right, Ms. Bannister. What you say makes sense. I'm not a gun control person, but I agree I don't want every Tom Dick and Harry packing pistols, which they may or may not know how to use properly, down the halls that my seventy-six year old mother is being wheeled down. I do have one more question. Suggestion, whatever you want to call it."

"Go ahead, Janet."

"Can't the hospital's rules about visitation be changed, just for the night. I don't want to leave Mama alone while this—this situation, or whatever else you want to call it—is going on. If somebody tries to get into her room, I want to be there, and I want my husband to be there. He weighs two-forty and he's got a black belt in karate. He doesn't need a gun. Just let this idiot try to get past him and see what happens."

Nina was about to answer this, when Lalima Singh appeared out of the crowd and made her way up the stairs. She was standing beside Nina when she said:

"I am Dr. Lalima Singh. I have met many of you, others I have not. But I must attempt to answer this question. Understand, the visitation rules are in place for a reason. There must be quiet in the corridors. It is vital that the patients in this hospital have the opportunity to sleep. Sleep is the most effective medicine of all. Our nurses and orderlies have duties to carry out, tests to continue to run, sometimes at two or three o'clock in the morning. Crowds of visitors during the night and early morning hours would make the execution of these duties even more difficult than they already are. Also, as I said, many of you, I do not know. Many of you our nurses and orderlies do not know. Strangers in the hospital—that is the one thing we must avoid."

She was silent for a time.

No one answered her.

No one even moved, until Nina ended sixth period assembly, saying:

"I need to go back up to my room now. And you all need to go home. Officer Rivard?"

Moon, who had been standing in one of the far corners:

"Yea."

"How many officers are here now?"

"Six. And I've called in two others to do town patrols, checking for anything suspicious."

"Do you feel that will be enough people?"

"I do. We'll have an officer at each entrance. Nobody gets in or out without our checking him out. There are four floors to the hospital, we'll have somebody on each floor patrolling the corridors and checking any rooms that might be empty. We're even gonna be checking the bathrooms."

Some laughter at this.

Nina quieted it:

"By morning this will all seem like a bad dream. Whoever is responsible for the explosion will either be gone or—even better—sitting in the Bay St. Lucy jail. But for now you have to trust your own hospital to be a place of safety and healing, and your police department to be capable of protecting you and your loved ones. Now school is over for the day. Everybody go home. And sleep well."

The crowd began to disperse, and the headlights that had made a parking lot in the front yard of the hospital began to disappear.

Lalima Sing put an arm around her waist and said quietly:

"That was masterfully done. You have my immense admiration."

"Well. You weren't bad yourself, especially dealing with the visitation situation."

A shake of the head:

"Visitors and family members at midnight. How utterly preposterous."

They were joined by Moon Rivard.

"Good job, Ms. Bannister. Was getting to be a bad situation."

"You did good too, Moon."

""Maybe so, maybe so. But to tell you the truth, I'm a little bit ashamed of myself."

"Why?"

"We're dealing with one young man, just one. If six trained officers can't do the job and catch this bird, we all ought to retire."

"I feel better already."

Lalima Singh:

"And we wish to ensure that you continue to feel better. Let us get you back in your room, and back on the IV. We might even wish to administer a mild sedative, so that you have at least some possibility of getting a bit of sleep tonight."

"I'm game. Although right now it seems hard to imagine. Going to sleep? I don't know if I'll ever get to sleep again."

Bridget O'Leary, who had just made her way through the crowd, laughed and said:

"You will, believe me. And I wanted to tell you: I heard your talk. It made me feel like I was back in high school. Good old Ms. Bannister, always in charge of the situation, then and now."

"Thank you, Bridget."

"Nothing to thank me for. But Dr. Singh, I do have a suggestion."

"And what would it be?"

"I think we should move Nina."

"Move her where?"

"To a room in the Intensive Care Unit."

"Why would you do this?" asked Moon.

Bridget:

"There are several rooms that might be more appropriate, but one in particular. It's right at the end of Corridor B."

Dr. Singh nodded:

"Yes, I know it. It's meant specifically for patients in recovery. There is high security in all of these corridors. Visitors are allowed in only rare cases, and for short times only. Camera surveillance. Even if no officers were to be in the room—which is unlikely—but even if this were the case, the room can be easily monitored from the front desk. There is much less coming and going of nurses, orderlies, cleaning staff. Yes. I think it a good plan."

"All right," said Bridget, nodding, "I'll make a call then and have the room prepared."

She left.

And within minutes, Nina was being wheeled into a different part of the hospital.

The halls and rooms were exactly as Lalima and Bridget had described them. The light was dimmer, the spaces were narrower, and the thick security doors more padded, more secure, more frequently splashed with yellow or bright red warning notices. She was wheeled by the central desk, and gave a little finger wave to Latricia who was sitting there. They were headed to a room in the corner. The half open doors she passed revealed quite often a family member sitting, motionless, by the bedside of a patient whose white and frizzled hair was all that could be seen protruding from a mass of blankets.

People here were very sick.

They were also very private. Few carts clattering down the halls. No nurses meeting each other and laughing raucously.

No one, Nina thought with satisfaction, is going to slip in here unseen.

They came to the door at the end of the corridor. Bridget unlocked it, swung it open, and wheeled Nina inside.

Where she immediately noticed that there was more large dinosaur-like equipment, more machines. The outer wall of the room, where the door opening was, was solid below, and with a wall window above. Curtains covered this window, and Bridget went to the window and pulled cords, separating the curtains and revealing the window. Bridget turned back to Nina, and said, "These curtains can be closed for more quiet, or open for more security—the nurse on duty can keep an eye on the patient that way."

After an uneventful ride up, they emerged into an equally uneventful, even deserted, hallway, at the end of which Nina saw her door open, her room beckoning, as well as her new bed.

A bed.

Sleep.

Could she sleep?

Maybe.

Sliding off the stretcher-cart, with Lalima on one side of her and Bridget on the other, she felt a bit ashamed that she had been afraid.

Oh face it—was afraid even now.

But that's ridiculous, Nina.

An entire police force is here protecting you. And protecting all of the other patients.

She got onto the bed and lay down.

She was on her back now. Bridget was preparing to re-insert the IV needle and Lalima Singh, standing just beyond, was preparing another shot that would contain, Nina assumed, some sort of a sedative.

"Okay," said Bridget, "let's get you back on this stuff. Little pin prick into this vein now."

"Nina!"

A voice from the doorway. She propped herself up in the bed.

And saw Frank standing there, shaking his head.

Almost involuntarily she shouted:

"Frank, what is it?"

This caused Lalima Singh to look at her for an instant, then at the IV bag.

A scream:

"No!"

The doctor then hurled herself at Bridget, crashing down upon the bed and knocking loose the IV tube, which Nina could now see dangling in the air.

She, Dr. Singh, and Bridget lay in a kind of human knot.

Bridget:

"What's the matter? What's happening?"

But Lalima Singh had disentangled herself, was now standing upright, and had begun to detach from its upright stand the clear plastic bag that held the IV liquid.

"What is it, Dr. Singh?"

"Ring the main desk downstairs. Tell them to find Officer Rivard and send him up here immediately."

"But..."

"I said immediately!"

"But what do I tell him?"

"I have to go now! But when he gets here, I shall be back. And I shall certainly at that time know what to tell him."

So saying, she left the room with the bottle gripped tightly under her right arm.

Bridget, on the phone now:

"This is Nurse O'Leary. Is Officer Rivard down there? Really? Put him on, please."

Pause.

Then:

"Officer Rivard? This is Bridget O'Leary. You need to get up here to Nina's room! No. No there's nobody here that we can see. When we got here, the room was empty. No, I'm not sure what the problem is. But Dr. Singh just left the room, really worried, and told me to call you. Yes. Quick as you can. All right."

She hung up.

"What is it, Bridget?"

"I don't know. But Nina, you shouted something to 'Frank.' What was that about?"

"Nothing, it's just. I have these fantasies sometimes. It's hard to explain."

They sat for a time, neither of them knowing what to say.

Two minutes later, Moon Rivard arrived, and, close behind him, Lalima Singh.

She was breathing hard, attempting to maintain her composure.

"What's happened, Dr. Singh?" asked Moon.

She could only shake her head.

Bridget walked over to her, put a hand on her shoulder, and squeezed. Then she asked softly:

"What was in that IV bottle?"

Another shake of the head, then the whispered words, to Bridget and Moon:

"Perhaps the three of us should talk outside."

Nina sat up in the bed:

"No. No. I want to hear this. What did Bridget almost put into me?"

"I—I thought looking at the bottle that something was wrong. The liquid in the IV bag should be clear. Look! It's gray."

"Bridget gasped, "The Gray Death!"

"'Gray Death'! What did Bridget almost inject me with, Dr. Singh?"

And then, Lalima Singh, looking straight at her, said:

"We won't know until it is analyzed what it is, but Bridget is possibly correct. We have been working with the police department about the opioid cases that we have seen increasing in the county. In one of our training sessions, Moon referred to the opioid solution as 'Gray Death.' This certainly looks like what he showed us, though I was reacting to the change of color, without thinking what it might be."

At that moment, Frank appeared in the doorway and said, quite audibly to Nina but to no one else:

"Not yet, Nina. Not yet."

Then he disappeared.

CHAPTER NINE: THE LETTER
7:35 P.M.

There was silence in the room for a time.

Nina spoke, her voice almost a whisper, "What would that have done to me?"

Dr. Singh shook her head.

Nina, a second time, this time her voice a little stronger:

"What would that have done to me? I want to know."

"All right. Gray Death is a mixture of different drugs like fentanyl and carfentanil—different combinations and strengths—making it a drug more potent than heroin. The effects of the drug are not metastasized in the body. It goes straight to the brain—the part of the brain that regulates breathing causing respiratory depression and death."

"That means…"

"You would have died within the hour."

More silence.

No one seemed to have anything to say.

A minute later, Michael Yancy entered the room, with a letter in his hand:

"One of the nurses downstairs gave me this letter, boss. She said somebody in the crowd downstairs gave it to her. It's addressed to you."

"All right, let's have it. Who did you say gave it to you?"

"One of the nurses. She said somebody in the crowd handed it to her. She had taken it up to Nina's old room.

But when she learned about the change she gave it to me."

"You ask her who that 'somebody in the crowd' was?"

"Yes, sir. She said it was a man. She didn't recognize him. But there were so many people downstairs—"

"Well, let's take a look at it."

He ripped open the envelope and took from it a neatly folded sheet of stationary. He read the letter, which Nina could see had been neatly typed.

"What is it, Moon? What does it say?"

He shook his head.

She persisted:

"Nobody wants to tell me anything. I came within a second of getting Gray Death shot into my veins. Whatever's in the letter can't be much worse than that. Let me see it."

He handed it to her. She read aloud:

"This letter is for Nina Bannister. The note in the locket was for you, Nina. In the bad times, the terrible times, when my father was about to take his life—in those times you were the only one who cared, the only one who helped us. So I ask you now, tell our story and try to find out who took that fifty thousand dollars. You had a chance just a few minutes ago, with the television cameras running. You were right there before the microphones. The television report could have been heard by hundreds of thousands of people. But you said nothing. Just that it was all an 'ongoing investigation.' I will never hurt you, Nina, not you personally. But I have had to do something to make you take your job seriously—and that job is to make Bay St Lucy realize my father was innocent."

This was the letter that Nina read aloud, with a voice much calmer than she had expected it to be when she started reading.

She finished, then shook her head and said:

"He said he would never hurt me; but he tried to kill me with Gray Death."

Moon shook his head:

"No, ma'am. He didn't know you'd be in this room. The opioid solution was to be for the next patient brought in here, whoever it might have been."

"Yes, I see that. But what did he mean about 'doing something' to make me tell his story?"

"I don't know. I guess we just have to wait and see."

And so they sat and looked at each other.

Finally Lalima Singh:

"So far as I can ascertain, this changes nothing. Clearly the letter was written by a human being and not a ghost. We have no idea where the man is now, but he is certainly not invisible. I am checking every few minutes with the nurse's stations, as well as individual nurses and orderlies on each floor, all going into and coming out of each individual room. Nothing amiss. And as for our situation here, it remains the same. The patients cannot simply be sent home, nor can the professionals who care for them."

Moon, gruffly:

"You're right, doctor. The only thing to do is catch this bird. That's my job. And Yancy, that's your job and the job of all the other cops we got staked out here. The main thing is, we got to…"

Lalima Singh's phone buzzed. She flipped it open, listened for a time, then looked at Nina and said:

"Do you know someone whose name is 'Towler'?"

"Of course. That's Edie Towler. She's been mayor here for several years. She's also on the hospital's Board of Directors."

"I see. Well, it seems she is calling from downstairs. She seems quite distraught. She wishes to come up and speak with you."

"Tell them to let her come up."

"All right."

Some seconds later, after flipping shut the phone, she said:

"Ms. Towler wishes to have all of the information that is available to us."

"Well," said Nina, "she's on the board. I'm sure they've all seen the television broadcasts, and they want to know what's going on. I can't blame them for..."

She was interrupted by the entrance of Edie herself, Edie dressed professionally, as always, this time in a beige business suit set off by a dark blue scarf.

Nina sat up in the bed and spoke first:

"Edie, I think I know why you're here. The board must be going crazy. We've just been holding on to some vital information that Moon and the police think ought to remain confidential. If you'll sit down we'll tell you everything that's happened so maybe you can inform the other board members and..."

But Edie merely shook her head and, in a quivering voice, said:

"To hell with the board, Nina. I think my father's been murdered."

CHAPTER TEN: EDIE
7:50 P.M.

Moon and Lalima were on one side of the bed, Edie the other.

"Edie," said Nina, "sit down. What's happening?"

Edie Towler could not sit down, but began to walk in a tight circle around the room. It was obvious that she was fighting back tears.

"Tell me what you know! Tell me what in God's name is happening here!"

Nina sat up and pulled the pillow down over the small of her back, saying:

"Edie, some of what we know has already been reported on T.V."

"Yes, I know. I saw that. But tell me the rest!"

"All right. Attached to the body found in the burning car was a metal locket. Inside the locket was a note saying, "Remember Cory Morgan.""

Edie put her hands over her face and sobbed.

"Oh no," she said, "this can't be happening!"

"What can't be happening? And how is your father involved?"

"Nina, you know my father was on the hospital board for some years. In a way I'm on it now because I inherited his position."

"Yes, I knew that."

Edie pulled the chair across the room and put her hand on the guardrail of the bed, leaning forward as she said softly, "Well, half an hour ago or so, I got a call from someone claiming to be Cory Morgan. He said my father was dead, was the body they found in the back seat of the burning car!"

"Oh no. Surely that can't be."

"I don't know. I just know Daddy was on the board during the whole scandal with Harrison Morgan. He was a leader of the faction that refused to give an inch, and that insisted on jail time for what he called a clear case of theft."

"Yes. I knew that."

"This caller said that everyone on the board at that time would pay. And everyone connected with the hospital."

"What did the caller sound like, Ms. Towler?" Moon interjected. "Could you recognize the voice if you heard it again?"

"No," she shook her head, "it was low and raspy, much like the caller was speaking into a rag or trying to disguise his voice."

Nina spoke up, "Have you tried to contact your father since the call?"

"Yes and I can't find him! You know he's lived alone in our original old two-story house out on Breakers Boulevard ever since Momma died. Well, I've just come from there. He's not at home. And that just doesn't make sense. He's eighty years old. He hates driving, even in good weather. But the car is gone. Where would he have gone tonight?"

Silence for a time.

Edie asked, with understandable urgency in her voice, "Moon, you have to tell me: the body that the reporter Chip Herndon described…"

"Yes, ma'am?"

"Have they learned anything more about it? Is it my father and you're just not telling me?"

Moon shook his head.

"No, ma'am. The body's at the morgue. They can't do a full autopsy until tomorrow morning. But I got to tell you—and this won't be easy on you."

"Go ahead. Say what you have to say."

"Well. Given the condition of that body, there won't be no fingerprints. The only thing they'll have to go by is…"

"I think I know."

"Yes, ma'am. The question is, who is your daddy's dentist?"

"Dr. Reinhard. Has been for years."

"Then, given the nature of that call, I think it might be a smart thing to contact Reinhard tomorrow morning first thing. We can do it if you'd like. We'll tell him there's a need for a full set of dental records, and that they need to be sent over to the morgue. Then, when they do the autopsy…"

But Edie shook her head.

"No. Is there a physician at the morgue now, preparing the body for tomorrow?"

"Yes, ma'am. I been talking to them over there every half hour or so to see if they've found anything we can use."

"All right. I'm not simply going to go home, lie down in my bed, and have a sound night's sleep while my father is…"

"Yes, ma'am, I understand."

"No. I know Dr. Reinhard well. I'm going to call him now at home."

"If that's what you want to do."

"It's not what I want to do; it's what I have to do. I'm going to beg him to meet me at his office. Then I'll sign for the records and take them to the morgue myself. There are fillings, metallic plates…it should be an easy thing to tell. And I have to know."

Nina exclaimed, "Edie, are you sure that's wise?"

"If it were Frank, would you wait all night to know?"

"I'd want to know, and I'd want to know right now. It's just that—well, there's something else."

"What else?"

Silence for a time.

Then Nina, quietly, "Edie, you're on the board too. He may come after you, too."

But Edie Towler only nodded, took a step toward the door and said, "I sincerely hope he does. If he's done anything to Daddy—oh yes, I sincerely hope he does."

And she walked out of the room.

CHAPTER ELEVEN: I LIKE YOUR HOUSE
8:00 P.M.

The next minute faded into the next five minutes which in turn faded into the next fifteen minutes. Nina was listening to Dr. Singh and to Moon—she was even talking—but she had no real idea of what she said or heard. There was something about keeping two guards at her door at all times. Something about assigning a car to follow Edie Towler as she went about her ghoulish errand at first the dentist's office then the morgue.

But a part of Nina's mind, possibly simply to maintain sanity, made it warm and light and summer.

She was having coffee with Margot at one of ten places that dotted the center of little Bay St. Lucy.

Coffee with just a ribbon of cream swirling on top, coffee that stood for sanity, coffee that kept the world tied together and making sense.

Coffee that would signal, as the rising sun would signal an end of this disastrous and nonsensical night.

Get through this, Nina, she told herself.

"Nina?"

This from Dr. Singh.

Answer her, Nina.

Answer.

"Nina, I can only imagine how you must feel now."

"I'm all right. I'm worried about Edie's dad. I'm worried about Edie herself. This man that we're dealing with—he seems to be everywhere and nowhere. But Dr. Singh—"

"Lalima. I am now to you Lalima and you are Nina. We shall, the two of us, get through this night together. And after we do so, we shall be close friends forever."

"I believe that too. It has to be true because you saved my life. If you hadn't seen the IV bag…"

She merely shrugged:

"What kind of a physician would I be if unable to differentiate Warfarin from a gray opioid solution?"

"It wasn't just that you recognized it. It was when you recognized it."

"You had shouted 'Frank.' It made me turn around, just in time. Who is Frank?"

"My husband."

"You saw your husband?"

"Yes."

"And he is dead?"

Nina merely shrugged.

And Lalima nodded:

"There are great mysteries. I am a scientist, yes. But I am also a Hindu."

Silence for a time. Then:

"Nina, the main thing is, you are all right. And I must make a suggestion to you, although you may find it distasteful after what you have just been through."

"What is it?"

"The sedative that I was to give you. I still think administering it would be wise."

"You're sure it's not Gray Death?"

A slight smile:

"You have my word. And it will not render you unconscious. It will merely relax you. Perhaps allow you to doze a bit."

"All right. If you think it's a good idea…"

"Yes. I definitely do."

Nina nodded, and accepted the small needle prick that went with the shot.

She began almost immediately to feel a drowsiness.

Lalima rose, squeezing her shoulder and smiling down at her:

"I must go now to check on patients. There are two officers outside your door. They will remain there all night. I shall send Judy by to check on you in a few minutes."

"Good."

And it was good.

The fuzziness in her brain intensified, in a pleasant and indescribable way.

She was back in the same coffee shop with Margot. No. No, the two of them were sitting in Elementals now, chatting about how much a certain painting should be priced. A bell was tinkling; Alanna de la Fosse entered, flamboyant as always, and the week ahead became dramatic. Tomorrow night a theatrical performance; Thursday evening chamber music at The Auberge...

It went on like that for a time.

Finally she was pulled back to reality by Judy, who was standing over her, holding out a cell phone:

"Ms. Bannister?"

"Yes?"

"A Ms. Towler has just phoned the hospital and asked to be transferred to you. This is one of our hospital phones. Dr. Singh was asked if you could be disturbed. She said that I should ask you if you feel like speaking on the phone."

"Yes. Yes, it's important. I'll take it."

She accepted the small phone and tried to make her mouth work normally as she spoke into it:

"Edie! How are you? Where are you?"

"I'm at Dr. Reinhard's office, Nina. He's been very nice about the whole thing and agreed to meet me here. He's getting the records now. Oh Nina..."

"I'm here, Edie."

"Nina, I'm so scared."

"I know."

"You don't mind if I call you, do you?"

"Of course not."

"I just feel very alone."

"You're not alone, Edie. Everyone in Bay St. Lucy is riding along with you."

There was a pause, then something like a laugh.

"Well, maybe not everyone in Bay St. Lucy—but at least everyone on the police force. There's been a patrol car following me ever since I left the hospital."

"Moon insisted. We just don't know who we're fighting here. And since you're on the board…"

"I know. Well—he's bringing the records out now. If you don't mind I'll call you from the…"

It seemed, Nina thought, *that she could not bring herself to say the word 'morgue.'*

So Nina said simply:

"You call as often as you want, Edie."

"Thank you."

And she hung up.

She then gave the phone back to Judy, saying:

"Ms. Towler is going to call back, probably quite soon. Would it be possible for you to leave the phone here on the table by the bed? Then we don't have to go through all these people and hurdles to get to me."

"I'm sure that will be all right, Ms. Bannister."

Judy left, and Nina was left with the evil phone, whose next ring she dreaded.

She could put herself in Edie's place now, driving in cold sleet to the much colder morgue.

Why wasn't this something that the police could handle?

But no—no, if this were possibly Frank, she herself, Nina and only Nina, would be making the drive across town with a seemingly innocuous package that could well have been a research paper on Shakespeare.

So for a time she simply allowed herself to drift back to Elementals. Margot was talking now, making plans to hang the works of a new painter in town. Then Alanna said something about a poetry reading and then...

...and then and then...

She must have dreamed this way for some minutes, she did not know how many.

When the phone buzzed.

How nice, those lovely days when phones actually rang and neither buzzed nor vibrated.

She picked it up and flipped it open, then said:

"Edie are you there? Can you tell anything?"

No answer.

"Edie, tell me what's happening! Tell me if..."

But there was only a hiss, which became a voice that said:

"Hello Nina. This is Cory Morgan. I like your house."

CHAPTER TWELVE: A CLEAR VIOLATION OF
HOSPITAL REGULATIONS
8:30 P.M.

The words chilled her and cut like a knife through
the soft mental curtain that had wrapped itself around
her brain.

She could think of nothing to say, and almost
certainly could not have made her tongue work if she
had thought of anything.

Instead, the voice continued, like the evening sea
tide moaning its way ever higher onto the beach.

"I…"

But there was nothing to say.

The tide rising, pulling sand pebbles along with it as
it rose and deepened.

"I was in your house. I'm not there now, but I was."
He chuckled. "You should have asked the police to
guard it. Of course, the police are guarding the hospital,
aren't they? Pity. They always seem to be where I'm
not. But as I say, I like your house a great deal. Oh and
by the way, I'm sending you a present. I hope you like
it. It should be arriving at any time now. When you
receive it, try to remember the letter I wrote you. And
remember: I had to do something to make you take
your job more seriously. Your job is to find out who
actually did steal the fifty thousand dollars they accused
my father of taking. And this is what I have done."

There was a click, then silence.

She waited for a time, then rang for Judy, who
quickly appeared in the doorway.

"Yes, ma'am?"

"Get Moon Rivard."

A shake of the head.

"I'm not precisely sure where he is right now."

"Just find him. And find Dr. Singh. I need them both here."

"I'll try, ma'am."

Judy disappeared into the corridor.

Her house.

He had been in her house.

Who were they dealing with? What were they dealing with?

Yet another nurse arrived, this one carrying a small pasteboard box.

"This was just found downstairs on a table by the reception desk. It has your name on it."

It did. The words *Nina Bannister* were neatly written in black ink.

It could have held a ring, or a pair of earrings.

She unwrapped the brown paper covering it and pulled open the box itself.

There was nothing in it except a weathered, narrow strip of leather perhaps six inches long.

In the middle of the strip was written the word FURL.

She looked at the collar for a second or so before anything went on in her mind. There was simply a blank space where thoughts or feelings or fears or anything else should be. Her hands were active, and her fingers gripped and loosened on the rather battered leather strip that lay within them.

Dr. Singh arrived first, then Moon.

They were speaking to her now, asking about the box and what it contained.

She could only shake her head.

Because the words: 'It's Furl's collar' would not come out.

She had to say it.

She couldn't face it without saying it.

So say it, Nina.

Go ahead.

"It's Furl's collar."

Moon asked, "Your cat?"

"Yes."

"But what is it doing in that…"

A few moments of silence while the thing sunk into the two people standing over her.

Nina split for a time into two people, one talking in the actual world of the hospital, the other talking, imagining, remembering…

…thinking of Furl.

Outside world Nina said quietly:

"He just called me."

"Who called you?"

"Cory Morgan."

"How did he manage to get through to you?"

"I told them to let the next call through. I was expecting it to come from Edie. She's…"

"Yes, Ms. Bannister, I know. She's at the morgue now. They're checking the dental records. Ought to have the results soon, and when they do, they'll call me. But this call you got…"

"Cory Morgan. He said he had been in my house. He said he was sending me a present. Then this arrived. It's Furl's collar. How could he have…"

And outside Nina went on talking—almost as though things were perfectly normal.

While inside Nina's brain…

Other things were going on.

She kept fingering the collar, turning it over and over, feeling mentally the warmth of Furl's neck, good

Furl who always closed his eyes and purred when Nina gently stuck an index finger between throat and neck and massaged the warm flesh.

Good Furl.

Moon was talking on his own phone now.

"Yancy? Hey, listen kid, you're the only one I can spare now. Get in a patrol car and drive over to Ms. Bannister's place. You know where it is?"

"Check, boss. You gave me the address a little while ago. Got it on my GPS. What am I looking for?"

"We think Cory Morgan may have been there in the last hour. Dumb of me not to order it watched, but we need everybody we can get here at the hospital. Now you be careful. See anything suspicious, call for backup. But if it looks clear, go in and look around. You may have to pick the lock. It's about a dollar eighty cent lock, so it shouldn't be that hard. And Yancy?"

"Yes, sir?"

"See if you can find the cat."

"The cat?"

"Yeah, be sure he's all right. His name is Furl."

Yes, that was true.

His name was Furl.

And now he was gone, she knew that.

Good Furl.

She could feel her throat begin to tighten. A tear had formed somehow in her left eye and was beginning its short trickle journey down over her cheek bone.

What had this man done to Furl?

And why? If he had some irrational hatred of the hospital, fine, but that could have had nothing to do with her. And even if it had, what had it to do with Furl?

She thought now of the body handcuffed in the back of the burning car. The body burned beyond all recognition. Is that what had happened to Furl? Had this monster poured gasoline on Furl, then lit a match and…

Outside and inside Nina came together; she heard her own voice saying:

"Furl is dead."

Moon assured her, saying, "We don't know that, Ms. Bannister."

"This creature burned a man to death. He handcuffed a man to the back seat door handle of a car, and then burned him to death. And he can be anywhere. He can be in my house. He can be in my hospital room…"

"We're going to catch him, Ms. Bannister. But we're going to just do one thing at a time. One thing, that's all. Right now we're going to wait for Yancy to tell us what he finds."

But Nina only understood one thing:

Furl was dead.

There was no more Furl.

All she could think about now was moving into her shack, a little more than sixteen years ago. She had walked to a nearby market to pick up some things for dinner that night. A movement had caught her eye, something following behind her.

It was a little, tan and white, lonely and bedraggled kitten.

Probably it had been abandoned on one of Bay St. Lucy's downtown streets. How it had caught sight of her she had no idea.

But there it was and there was nothing to do but pick it up and take it home with her.

The darned cat was always wanting her to slide the big glass door open so that he could go out on the deck; and once out on the deck the darned cat was wanting her to slide the door open so that he could come back in.

One of the neighbors—since moved away—had flown a flag religiously, running it up in the morning and taking it down at sunrise. Furl the flag, unfurl the flag.

Slide open the door, slide closed the door.

Open and close, Furl and Unfurl.

Ten years ago.

Furl had come into their lives about five years before Frank died—sixteen years, multiply times seven for human years. That made Furl over one hundred years now, well past Nina's age.

The tears were falling on her hospital gown now, like saliva that might have been dribbling on a baby's bib.

Of course it wasn't the same Furl, just as it wasn't the same Nina. He moved very slowly now, padding across the living room floor to greet her as she came home every evening. Not enough energy to jump up on the couch, let alone chase mice that somehow occasionally came up from downstairs.

But he was always there for her.

Furl, good Furl.

Moon was talking on the phone now.

Talking to Michael Yancy.

How much time had passed?

She did not know exactly; she had been in the past, playing with Furl.

But in that time, young Yancy had reached her shack, and was reporting in.

"Yancy? Tell me what's going on!"

Rasping static, then Michael's voice, "Yancy here."

"You there, son?"

"Just pulled up."

"What's it look like?"

"Hard to see from down here on the driveway. The sleet seems to be coming down even harder. It's rattling on the roof of the squad car and on the tin room of her shack. Sounds like machine guns are going off."

"Any cars there?"

"No. Driveway's empty. Listen, Moon, I'm getting out of the squad car now."

"Just be careful, you understand?"

No answer. Nina could hear the sound of the car door opening, then came louder sounds of wind and sleet.

Then Michael's footsteps.

She could hear him breathing.

Finally, he spoke, "Moon, I'm at the base of the stairway."

"You think you can pick the lock and get in?"

A pause.

Then:

"Moon?"

"Yeah?"

"I'm shining my flashlight up at the door to the shack."

"And?"

"Door's open. It's swinging in the wind, blowing open and then banging shut."

Moon did not speak for a time.

"Is there," he said finally, "a light on up there?"

"Yes. The living room light is on."

"Well. You got to go on up and take a look. Get your gun out."

"You don't have to tell me that. Okay. I'm heading up the stairs now."

She could hear the familiar sound of the steps creaking.

The third from bottom step; the step exactly halfway up...

...it was as though she were climbing them herself.

Then:

"All right, I'm going in now."

Another pause.

"Moon, I'm standing in the living room. There's nobody…wait a minute!"

"What? What's going on up there?"

But Yancy's voice, louder now, was not replying to Moon.

"Who's in there? Who's in the bedroom? Come out of there? Come out here or I'll shoot!"

"What's happening, Yancy?"

"I said I'll shoot! I'm a Bay St. Lucy police officer! You can't hide in there, whoever you are! Get out here! I'm going to count to three; if you're not out here by then, I'm coming in. And I WILL SHOOT YOU!"

"Yancy, what's…"

"ONE!"

"Son…"

"TWO!"

Then another voice was heard.

"It was a woman's voice, and she was crying, "Don't hurt me! Please don't hurt me!"

Nina recognized the voice.

It continued, "I'm Ms. Peterson. Lizzy Peterson. I'm Nina's neighbor!"

"All right, Ms. Peterson!" Yancy was saying now. "So what are you doing in Nina's house?"

"Well I…about half an hour ago, I heard someone walking up Nina's stairs. I thought it might be the police, but I didn't see a squad car in the driveway. Then I realized there was a car parked down by the beach, but it was too far away. With the sleet and all, I couldn't see it. So, I just waited."

"And?"

"I could hear somebody walking around. The walls of these shacks are thin. The light came on. The curtains were pulled shut though, and I couldn't see who it was, I couldn't see who was in there."

"Go on…"

"After a while I heard…and this really scared me."

"What did you hear?"

"I heard a kind of yowl from Nina's cat."

Silence.

Nina fought to keep from sobbing too loudly.

She tried not to imagine what was happening at that moment to Furl.

Good Furl.

Yancy was heard again, "Then what?"

"Nothing. Not until I heard the door again. The lights went off, and whoever it was went down the stairs. After a few minutes, I heard the sound of the car starting down near the beach. I waited a while and then…well, I thought I should come over and check. I did. The door was standing open; I knew that was wrong. So I thought I would go up and look around. I especially wanted to see if someone had tried to steal anything. And I wanted to check on Furl—that's Nina's cat."

"What did you find?"

"Not anything wrong. I come over to Nina's every now and then. Everything looked just like it was supposed to. Except…"

"Yes? Except what?"

"I can't find Furl."

Silence for a time.

Then Michael's voice saying, "All right, Ms. Peterson. Thank you for being a good neighbor. You can go home now."

"Can you tell me first about Nina? Is she all right? I saw her on T.V. from the hospital."

"Yes, ma'am. She's fine."

"But what's going on at the hospital? Is someone shooting over there?"

"No, ma'am. We've got it taken care of."

"Are you going to stay here at Nina's in case whoever this is comes back?"

"I don't know that. I'll have to talk with my boss. But as for now, it's like I say: I think it's going to be all right if you just go back home and try to get some sleep. If you hear anything else or see anything else just give us a call. Here's a card with my number on it. Just ask for Patrolman Yancy."

"Well, if you're sure…"

"We can't do much else, ma'am. Nothing's out of order here."

"But Nina's cat…"

"There's nothing we can do about that, either. There's no blood, and no sign that the animal has been hurt. The door was open. Maybe he just got out."

"Maybe, but…"

"I'll go downstairs and look around. But it's like I say: you should go back home and try to sleep. By morning we'll have all this taken care of."

"All right."

Nina could hear footsteps as Else Peterson left her house, opened and closed the door, then walked down the stairs.

Then Yancy on the phone, "Moon?"

"Yeah?"

"Did you hear all that?"

"We did."

"It's like I said. There's just nothing wrong here. No sign that anyone stole anything. No sign that the cat was…well, you know."

"I know."

"So what do you want me to do? Stay here?"

"No, son, I can't spare you. Besides I don't see any reason that whoever was there is going to come back tonight. You come on back here to the hospital."

"All right then. Over and out."

And the phone went silent.

Nina tried to speak, barely succeeded, "What has happened to Furl, Moon?"

"I don't know. It doesn't look good. Obvious somebody took him. What they did then, why…"

Moon's phone rang again.

"Moon here."

He flipped a switch on the intercom. Now Nina could not hear the voice on the other end.

Moon continued:

"Yeah. So what have you learned?"

Nina asked, "Who is it?"

"It's the morgue, Ms. Bannister."

Then back into the receiver:

"Did Ms. Towler arrive with those dental records? We had a man following her just in case. Yeah. Yeah. So you were able to run the check? Yeah, I understand. And then she left, Ms. Towler did? When was that? Okay, and she said she was coming over here? All right. She should be here any time now. And you're sure about the results? No chance of a mistake? All right, that's good work."

At that moment, Edie Towler burst into the room, threw herself on Nina, and began to sob.

Her face was pressed hard on Nina's chest, and her hands continually balled into fist and then opened again.

"Nina!" she was able to stammer. "Oh Nina!"

"It's all right. It's all right, Edie."

She looked at Moon, who had just pressed the 'off' button on his intercom.

"Moon…"

And he smiled back at her:
"It is going to be all right, Ms. Bannister."
"What do you…"
A simple shake of the head:
"It's not him."

It took Edie some moments to stop crying. When she finally did, she walked to one of the chairs near the bed and sat down.

"Nina, it was the hardest time I've ever spent, just sitting there in that awful place. So cold, and just white. What an awful place. I was in a waiting room. Every minute I knew the door would open and a man with a white coat would come out and shake his head and say, 'I'm sorry but I have to tell you…'"

"But it didn't happen that way, Edie."

"No, thank God. The door did open, and the man did come out. But he smiled first, before he talked, and I knew things were going to be all right. Two policemen came into the room with him, and one of them came over, squeezed my shoulder, smiled and said: 'Not a match, Ms. Towler. Not even close. Someone was trying to trick you. We still don't know who that burned body is, but it isn't your father.'" I broke out crying. I just wanted to come over here and tell you myself."

Moon:

"That's real good news, Ms. Towler. That's the best news we've had tonight. I gotta ask you though. About your father…"

But Edie only shook her head. She was laugh-crying now:

"No, it's all right. I was halfway over here when my cell phone buzzed. I flipped it open and thank God it was his voice."

"Your father's?"

"Yes! Someone had called him earlier and told him that I was out by Breaker's Point and had experienced car trouble, that he needed to go out there."

"Who called him?"

"He didn't find that out. The man just hung up. And Daddy, the way he is, rather than calling the police, just drove on out there. That's where he was when I came by his place."

It was at that moment that Bridget O'Leary entered the room and said:

"Nina, someone downstairs wants to see you."

Lalima Singh turned to her and said, "I am not certain, Nurse O'Leary, that Ms. Bannister is in the condition to see anyone right now. I have given her a sedative, which has not helped terribly much to calm her during the last few moments."

"I think she'll want to see this visitor. In fact, actually, he's on his way up right now."

"You did this without asking my permission?"

"Trust me. You'll be happy I did. You will be too, Nina."

Nina could only shake her head.

"If you think I need to see this person, Bridget…"

"I didn't say it was a 'person.' But here he is, anyway!"

And it was true. A very young nurse that Nina had not seen before was entering the room with a blue travel bag, within which was wriggling and yaaowing a tan and white Furl.

"I tried to carry him," she said, smiling, "but he wouldn't let me. He kept biting and scratching. Somehow we got him in here, packed in with towels around him."

"Furl! Oh Furl!"

"We just found him downstairs. Someone must have dropped him off just outside the front door of the ER.

They heard him meeowing, trying to get in out of the cold. When one of the nurses went out to get him, there was a little yellow note stuck to his tail. It said, 'Please give Nina her cat.' They called me, thinking I might be able to run down whatever car must have dropped him—but there was nothing.

The bag was turned upside down and Furl dropped out of it and onto Nina, whom he started licking like a dog while he purred.

"What happened to you? Did somebody hurt you?"

"He seems fine," said the nurse, continuing to smile but obviously a bit shaken by her encounter with the strictly one-owner Furl, whom even Nina herself could not put into a cat carrier without the use of a plumber's helper. "We had one of the doctors who was just coming on shift look at him and give him a quick examination. Nothing broken, doesn't appear to have any digestive issues. Hasn't eaten anything that might hurt him."

Furl had his eyes closed now, and was shaking his head while Nina rubbed it.

"Thank you," she said, ostensibly to the nurse but actually to God.

"Thank you, thank you for making Furl be okay. I couldn't...without Furl, I just couldn't..."

"It's all right, Nina," said Bridget. "You've got him back. Nobody's hurt him. There's just one problem though."

"What?"

"He can't stay in the hospital. Strict rules about that."

"Oh. I guess that would be right. Listen Moon..."

"Yes, ma'am?"

"Do you have Jackson Bennet's phone number?"

"Sure do. He gave it to me just before he left here with his daughter."

"Jackson often keeps Furl. He's done it several times in the last few months. Furl trusts the Bennets and likes being over there. Jackson's probably just getting home now…"

"You want me to call him?"

"If you would."

"Course I will."

Bridget to the nurse:

"Why don't you take him downstairs until Mr. Bennet comes to pick him up? Every doctor on the duty roster will have my…well, will be mad at me if they see an animal in intensive care."

"Yes, ma'am."

It was with some difficulty that Furl was repacked, but he tolerated the separation as well as Nina did: with hurt feelings but still an understanding of the situation.

He was taken from the room, his yowls a bit softer now.

As were Nina's.

CHAPTER THIRTEEN: HOPE IS HERE!
9:00 P.M.

A brief moment elapsed when the room was full of smiles and mutual congratulations. Edie's father was all right, as was Furl.

But the moment could not last, of course, since the creature calling himself Cory Morgan was still either on the streets of Bay St. Lucy or in the hallways (or rooms or closets) of the hospital.

Nina was hardly surprised then when Edie addressed Moon with darker undertones in her voice, even despite the gracious content of her words:

"Moon," she said, seating herself near him and looking down a bit ashamedly at her lap, "Moon, I'm sorry to have put you and your men to so much trouble."

He merely shook his head:

"You got nothing to be ashamed about, Ms. Towler. Why if it was me in your place, I'da done the same thing. I'da been scared to death and would'a wanted to know one way or another. We don't know who we're dealing with here, but it's pretty obvious he's getting a big kick out of this, and that he's clever as hell. He seems to be everywhere at once, and nowhere at all."

Edie paused, then nodded as she said:

"I know, Moon, I know. That's why…"

Short pause as though she hardly knew what to say next. Moon interjected:

"Ma'am—what is it you're trying to say?"

"Something that isn't easy to say. Not at all easy."

"Then take your time. But I imagine you need to get it said. Whatever it is, it couldn't be much worse than some of the other things we've all had to hear tonight. Ain't nobody dead that we didn't already know about, is there?"

"No, Moon, as far as I can tell there are no new deaths. But we don't want there to *be* any more deaths and that's why..."

"Yes, ma'am. Go on."

"That's why we...oh God, I hardly know how to say this. I feel like I'm betraying my best friend. But you have to understand: after the second television broadcast, I began getting call after call from the other board members. They insisted on knowing what you were doing to solve the problem, to catch this maniac and make the hospital safe again."

"I understand that."

"And more and more of them began pressuring me to do what I didn't want to do. What I would only have done as a very last resort."

He was silent for a time, then he looked down at the floor and growled.

"They been after you to fire me, is that it?"

"Not fire you exactly but..."

"But bring in somebody else. Somebody better."

"Moon, it's been getting worse for the last hour. First the suggestion came from just a few of them. Then they began talking with each other. There was talk of a late night emergency meeting. They were going to replace me as head of the board if I didn't call and request help from..."

"From the Mississippi State Police up in Jackson."

To this she only nodded.

Silence in the room for a time.

"Well," Moon finally said, "I'm not all that surprised. One kid, terrorizing the whole town, the whole hospital, and I can't catch him."

"It's not as though we all don't…"

"Trust me, I know, but…"

He was interrupted by the buzzing of his walkie-talkie.

He flipped a switch and said into the receiver:

"Moon here. Yeah. Yeah I'll talk to him."

He got up and took a step toward the door, saying to both Nina and Edie, "This is Captain Hall calling from Jackson. I'm about to get officially relieved. Probably reamed out a bit too. I better leave the room to take this."

So saying, he turned to leave the room, pulling the door open and letting it shut soundlessly behind him.

Edie was silent for a time, then said quietly, "I'm so sorry about this."

Nina ran her fingers through her hair, then shook her head and said, "It isn't your fault. Moon's right about one thing: the town is terrified. The hospital is its nerve center. It can't be abandoned. But as things are now, it also can't be trusted as a safe haven."

Judy entered, saying, "You have a visitor, Ms. Bannister. They told her about visiting hours being over, but she says it's urgent. Something about information she's got, and that she has to share with you. She won't go. And since she's so old, the police don't want to risk hurting her."

"Who is this visitor?"

"She says her name is…"

"Hope, dear. My name is Hope."

And indeed it was.

For there in the doorway had just appeared the diminutive figure of Hope Reddington.

She had been often referred to around Bay St. Lucy as The Hope Diamond. It was a comparison not precisely accurate, for although the lady now standing before them was slightly smaller than the jewel of the same name, she was much brighter, and she possessed many more facets, from which a startling kind of radiance seemed always to be emanating. She was harder, too, or at least she would have had to be, given certain things that had happened in her past. Her husband, Marshall Reddington, owner of the town's largest pharmacy—and for a time Nina now remembered—member of the hospital's board of directors, had been rumored to be involved in shady dealings with that shadiest of characters, Homer Baron Robinson, a year or so before the man's assassination—by his own daughter as it ultimately turned out, and not by New Orleans gamblers, as had been originally supposed. That was bad enough. But when the rumors began to subside and life for the Reddingtons had begun to return to some semblance of normalcy, Marshall had been stricken by a cruel form of cancer and forced to wither in their stately home until quite mercifully delivered to the grave. In the year following, her daughter and son-in-law, quite happily married, were killed in an automobile accident, leaving a daughter of their own, Helen, who, herself, suffered from three insidious diseases: the first beauty, the second talent, and the third (the only one of the three to prove invariably incurable and unfalteringly fatal) success.

But if Hope did not quite spring eternal, then she at least bubbled forth in a dogged mortality, coming as near to timeless as humanity, in its white tight ringlet-haired stooped caned hearing-aided ninety-genarian, but who cares and damn the next century form—could manage.

"Hello, Nina and Edie."

"Hope!" exclaimed Nina. "Hope it's so good of you to come. But it's so late! Did Helen and John bring you?"

"No. I called a cab. I had been watching the television. After the second broadcast, the one mentioning Cory Morgan, I felt I had to come."

Hope began making her way into the room. She was, Nina remembered while watching her approach, always looking up and out from under something. This had not been hard in, say, Margot's shop, because there was always something or other—a painting, a vase, an ashtray, a pot, a bouquet, an engraving—to be looking up and out from under.

But Hope simply lived her life looking up and out from under something even if nothing was there, as was the case in this spare hospital room.

She finally reached a chair, sat, folded her bat-like hands in front of her, and said to Edie Towler:

"Edie, it's so good to see you."

"And it's good to see you, too, Hope. It's been far too long."

"Yes, it has. We used to see each other more often, I know, but I don't get around too much anymore."

"Then I shall come to see you."

"Yes, I should like that very much. You're here I suppose because of your love for Nina and also your position. You are still president of the hospital board?"

"Yes. For the time being anyway."

"And for much longer I should hope. The hospital is fortunate to have you. Marshall, as you may remember, was on the board before his illness."

"I remember that. I was just a little girl, but I remember your husband so well. He used to give me candy when I came into the pharmacy."

"He was a kind man, and a good one. But yes, Edie, we must talk more, and catch up on old times. And whenever you can come by, I would love to see you. Helen and John spend a great deal of time with me. But it still gets lonesome in a big old house."

"I'm sure it does."

In the momentary silence that followed, Nina allowed her mind to wander back to that "big old house," and to the days when she and Frank—newly married then—would be invited over for dinner, sitting outside in the yard during the warm summer nights.

Hope and Marshall, approximately ten years older and raising a young daughter, were somehow the models of a perfect marriage.

And that house, that house—

—she had always loved it.

As well as the neighborhood.

A few years after their marriage, when Frank's law firm had begun to enjoy at least some success, the two of them had bought a house in the same section of town.

It was not the most elegant and expensive neighborhood of Bay St. Lucy. There were no mansions here. The trees were not as stately and magnificent and the people were not as stately and magnificent. But both the trees of this neighborhood and the people of this neighborhood had done all right for themselves. They were upper middle class trees and people, who exuded in comfort and conviviality what they might have lacked in lineage and wardrobe. They shaded each other. Low to the ground, hard-working and efficient, they shared a flora/fauna appreciation for cracked-with-time sidewalks, ambulatory and not decorative. The trees shaded these sidewalks not because they were obligated by God to do so but because the sidewalks seemed to attract them down, invite them as it were.

And the people on these sidewalks shared something in common with the trees themselves. Not passing helter-skelter over the concrete on their way to some encounter or another but standing rooted in it, as the sun set, and they chatted aimlessly about the turning of the earth.

This was Bay St. Lucy at its best.

Character, morals—Bay St. Lucy at its best.

"There is something," Hope finally said, "that I need to tell both of you. It concerns this young man Cory Morgan."

"Yes?" replied Nina.

"The fact is, his father did not steal fifty thousand dollars from the hospital's operating budget."

"How do you know that, Hope?" asked Nina.

"Because my husband did."

CHAPTER FOURTEEN: A DEAL WITH THE DEVIL
9:20 P.M.

If it had been day, and the sun had been out, it would have stopped still in the sky.

But that event, if one believes biblical sources, had already happened.

A recurrence would not have been nearly as shocking as the assertion by Marshall Reddington's wife that her husband had stolen fifty thousand dollars.

There was only one appropriate comment to be made, or rather one fitting and proper question to be posed. Nina thought for a time, formulated it, and asked it:

"What?"

Hope glanced around the room for a second or so in search of something to look up and out from under, found nothing, and so contented herself simply by saying:

"Yes. I'm sure you understood me. He took fifty thousand dollars from the hospital's operational budget, then let Harrison Morgan take the blame for it."

"But that," said Edie, "is incredible!"

"Nevertheless."

Nina, attempting to sound somewhat rational, was only able to stammer out:

"Hope, you mustn't say such things."

"What things, Nina dear?"

"Why things that could not possibly be true!"

"But these things are true."

"Hope, your husband was one of the finest men I ever knew."

"And one of the finest," Hope replied, "that *I* ever knew. I was so lucky to have him in my life."

Edie, leaning forward a bit now in her chair:

"Your husband couldn't possibly steal anything, let alone fifty thousand dollars."

Nina, chiming in, "And if he did—which, as Edie just said, he never would—he would never let someone else take the blame for it and go to prison."

A pause.

The sun, albeit shining now in Asia Minor, remained stationary in the sky.

It was difficult to continue this conversation, which was not really a 'conversation' as such but a string of exclamations.

Life lived and narrated in exclamation points.

One of the two women—it hardly mattered which—said slowly and softly, even conspiratorially:

"Hope you can't go on talking like that. People will think you're—"

"Demented?"

"No, of course not. But…"

Hope merely smiled and said, "They think I'm demented now. I myself think I'm a little bit demented. Perhaps more than a little bit."

"Listen, you have to understand," Nina replied, "there is so much tension in this hospital, in this town. The messages, the phone calls, the letters, the burned body—if you say that Marshall stole that money, somebody might actually believe you."

"I want somebody to believe me."

"But what you're saying is absurd! It didn't happen!"

"Oh but it did happen!"

"How?"

Hope sat quite still for a time, then closed her eyes and went back in time.

"We had been in Bay St. Lucy for some years. Our daughter was eight. The pharmacy was doing well, and Marshall had been for almost two years on the hospital's board of directors. But he had also come under the influence of Homer Baron Robinson."

"What," asked Nina, "would he have had in common with that gangster?"

And even as she asked the question, her own mind drifted back in time.

The Robinsons. An immensely wealthy family. Roots quite shady. Not a Creole name nor even a Mississippi one. Robinson the autocrat standing quite solitary on the balcony of his mansion, looking out over Breakers Boulevard and over the sea beyond.

"What," asked Nina again, even more incredulously, "could Marshall have had in common with that man?"

"Gambling."

It was Edie's turn now to be incredulous as she sat forward on her chair and said, "I always thought Marshall had no vices."

But Hope merely shook her head and said:

"There are no men with no vices."

Then she continued, "—and probably no women either."

To which Nina could not stop herself, lover of Henry Fielding as she was, from whispering, "We are all as God made us. And some of us, much worse."

Hope sighed resignedly and said, "Not very much worse, not my Marshall. But a little. A little. And as for vices, well, I suppose we would have to add one more to his list."

"That one being?" asked Nina.

"Ambition. He wanted to 'be' somebody in Bay St. Lucy, as though that would have meant anything to me.

Or to his daughter. But Homer Robinson was the most powerful force in the town. No one was appointed to anything or elected to anything, without his say. It was his influence that got Marshall appointed to the hospital board. At any rate, for some reason he took a liking to my husband, who felt flattered by it, and somehow excited by the power the man exuded. Once or twice a week he would play poker late into the night at the mansion, with people—well, I never knew exactly which people. But not from here. Not from Bay St. Lucy."

"Did he win at these games?" asked Edie.

"At first he did. At first. But now looking back after all those years, I believe he was only being lured in. Or 'set up,' as they say."

"So what happened next, Hope?" asked Nina.

But even as she asked the question, she sensed the difference in her own tone. She was no longer incredulous, unbelieving. This was not a demented woman raving about something that never could have happened.

No, this did happen.

In her Bay St. Lucy.

To people she had loved, and still loved.

All these things she realized as she repeated the question, "What happened next?"

To which Hope merely shrugged, a wan smile much like a cloud-covered sun playing across the features of her face.

"What had to happen, I suppose. The nightly card games at the Robinson Mansion turned into long weekends in New Orleans. 'Business trips,' I was told. Meetings with 'city officials' from around the state, in order to discuss financial matters that might be important for Bay St. Lucy. I was only given the vague outlines of such meetings. But I, country girl that I was, shared in Marshall's guilt, his duplicity. I was not immune to visions of grandeur. I was madly in love with the owner of a pharmacy. But if that man could become a city leader, or perhaps something more—how exciting!"

"But that was not," interjected Edie, "what actually happened."

"No. What happened was that Marshall, whether at the track or in expensive rooms in The Monteleone Hotel, was gambling with ever larger sums of money. There began to be strange phone calls. The evenings he was here, he could never seem to fall asleep. There were complaints from pharmacy customers, mistakes in the filling of prescriptions."

"And finally?"

"Finally came the surprise audit. The hospital was short fifty thousand dollars."

"Which Harrison Morgan was accused of taking."

"And which he never touched. He was completely innocent all along. Homer Robinson engineered the audit, had it carried out at his orders. He also saw that it was carried out by 'auditors' from New Orleans, who were little more than gangsters themselves, or at least the stooges of gamblers. But whoever they were, they were good at their jobs. They made it look as though Harrison Morgan was the only one who possibly *could* have taken the money."

A small and acid silence ensued, during which time the room and all its furnishings, as well as the three people assembled in it, prepared to hear the question that now had to be asked.

And it was asked of course. It hardly mattered by whom.

The interrogator could just as well have been the radiology tube that sat gray and dormant in the corner.

"Hope?"

"Yes?"

"Hope, the two of you knew that Harrison Morgan was not guilty?"

"Yes."

The next question could only have been asked by Nina.

And it was:

"All the time Frank was trying to defend him, you knew him to be innocent?"

"Of course we did."

"Then why—in heaven's name why—"

"Why did we say nothing?"

Neither Edie nor Nina could ask the question in such a way that it included that fateful word.

Nothing.

Nothing.

So they simply waited and asked:

Nothing.

Letting Hope continue telling the story, unravelling the string.

"The news broke concerning the audit. That night Marshall and I did not sleep. He told me the truth about the gambling debts. I was—well, I suppose you can form some idea of how I felt. Within the space of a few hours, the life we had built was falling apart around us. But finally at around three in the morning—I remember it as though it were yesterday—we both simply knew. It simply came to us and we knew. We would both go to the police the first thing in the morning and tell them everything. If it meant prison then it meant prison, but it was the only conscionable course of action. I did not know the Morgans well, neither of us did. They had not been long in Bay St. Lucy. But they were good people. And they were innocent."

"But why had your husband agreed to this scheme in the first place?"

"There were threats coming out of New Orleans. Threats that he himself might be jailed if he did not 'go along' with the scheme. But once we talked it through, really talked it through—we realized that we could survive it. As a couple, believing in each other, we could survive it. And if he had to be sent to jail for unpaid debts, why so be it."

"The next morning though, you didn't go to the police."

"No."

"Why not?"

"Because when we woke up we found a package at our door. Small, brown, neatly wrapped, and addressed to our eight-year-old daughter, with the words 'To be opened by her mother,' on it. So I opened the package. In it was picture of our daughter, playing in the yard. There was also a white lily. And there was also a human finger."

"My God."

"I think those were my words, dear—but God did not seem to be listening, and if he had been listening, I'm not certain where his sympathies would have lain."

"They threatened to kill you."

"They threatened to kill first our daughter. Then—as we learned only a short time later—me. And finally Marshall. All in horrible ways."

"But why," asked Edie, "did these mobsters care who took the blame for stealing the money? Harrison, Marshall—what did it matter to them, as long as they got their money?"

"This was what we asked ourselves at first. But that morning a car arrived for Marshall. A big black car. Mr. Robinson would like to meet with him. Over breakfast. My husband went of course. He was back almost within the hour. A short meeting. But in it several facts were made clear. Namely, as far as Mister Robinson was concerned—as well as his associates in New Orleans—this matter was closed. Harrison Morgan had stolen the money and that was the end of the matter. If Marshall had confessed, then he would naturally have been interrogated as to why he had stolen the money. Why, to pay gambling debts. Debts to which gamblers?"

"Gamblers," Nina whispered, "who did not want to be named."

"And who did not, at least in the eyes of the law-abiding world, and the sparkling sand beaches of Bay St. Lucy, did not even exist."

Silence for a time. Nothing could be heard except some murmuring and soft laughter from the nurse's station.

Then Hope continued, "During the trial we continued to agonize over the matter. We watched the Morgan family suffer. Their world was falling apart just as ours had appeared on the brink of falling apart. We thought, if we turned the matter over to the police, we could be protected."

"You could," Edie said quietly, "be protected from the New Orleans branch of the Mafia by young Moon Rivard and the Bay St. Lucy police force."

"That seemed to be our choice. We also thought that if we confessed and Marshall were sent away, the two of us could move somewhere else. Somewhere they…"

"Would not find you," said Nina, then adding, "but, of course, they would find you."

"Yes. There would be no place to hide."

Somewhere in the distance could be heard the faint howl of a siren.

Hope continued her tale in a steady voice, saying, "The verdict came, and almost immediately thereafter the shocking suicide. The boy Cory and his mother moved away. We did not know where. No one seemed to know where. And so, after that, confessing…"

Edie interrupted and said, "…would have seemed pointless. Whom would it have helped? It would not have brought back Harrison Morgan. Or made the lives of his widow and son the least bit easier."

"That was the way we reasoned. And so we simply kept quiet. We had done a horrible thing. And we knew it. Life went on, but it was never the same. A year after the trial, Marshall learned of his cancer. It was hard to believe, watching him suffer, that this pain was not some kind of divine retribution. He died. But we had ruined three lives not just one. Sometimes justice moves slowly. But there came the accident. Our daughter and her husband were killed, as you know."

Pause for a while. Edie and Nina remained silent.

"Now there is only me. Helen and John, well— perhaps the bill has been paid. At least, that is what I had been forcing myself to believe these long years. And now Cory has returned. The crime goes on and on. The cycle does not end."

And so, with that, the sun began its movement across the world's wide blue skies again.

But it was not quite the same sun.

It never is.

CHAPTER FIFTEEN: ADIEU JANE AUSTEN
9:35 P.M.

Something had to be done or said.

Something had to be done or said after World War II or Hiroshima.

Basically the same thing here.

So go on in there, Nina, and say what had to be said; do what had to be done.

"Hope, I don't know what to say."

Well, that isn't quite 'saying what has to be said,' is it?

"I'm just so sorry."

Not much better.

Stop trying and just listen.

"I know, dear."

"That you should have had to live with this for all these years..."

"As a fraud. As a fraud."

"How can you mean that?"

"All of those church services, passing as a decent Christian..."

"You are a decent Christian."

"I'm the worst kind of sinner."

"We're all sinners, Hope."

Hope slightly trembled and said, "Not like I am. I am a blight to the community."

"Hope, don't talk that way. Your life was in danger. All of your lives were in danger."

"We should have risked those lives. Rather than sacrificing others—yes, we should have risked those lives."

"That's easy to say. But how many people in Bay St. Lucy—or anywhere else for that matter—would have acted differently?"

"Two people would have."

"Which two people, Hope?"

"You would have. And Edie, you would have."

Both women merely shook their heads, but it remained for Nina to admit:

"I don't know, Hope. I honestly don't know."

Something like a smile passed across Hope's features as she said, "Then that is your great blessing. I do know. And that has been my great curse."

Silence for a time.

Then Edie, the organizer, the leader, the president of all groups.

Edie, the Active, said, "Hope, what do you want to do with this information? What do you want Nina and me to do?"

"I want you to tell the truth. Tell the truth that I have been too cowardly to tell all these years."

"Tell it how? To whom?"

"I believe the newsman's name is 'Herndon,' is it not?"

"Chip Herndon. Yes, he's been covering the story," Nina confirmed. "He's the one who's been on the television?"

"Yes."

"And you can contact him?"

"Yes, I'm sure we can. He's been wanting to talk to me every hour or so this evening anyway."

"Then he should in fact talk to you. Because now you have something to say. A news story, a true news story involving people's lives. Yes, my dear friend Nina—now you do indeed have something to say."

Edie chimed in, "But what are you going to do, Hope?"

Hope took a big breath and sighed, "I'm going home. My taxi is waiting. I'm tired. I'm going home, where, for the first time in oh such a long while—I shall finally be able to sleep. Truly sleep."

"But Hope, what about Helen and John?" asked Nina. "This news is going to devastate them. Do you want them to hear about it on the midnight news?"

"No, of course not. But there is no choice."

"If Nina and I don't tell Chip Herndon tonight…"

"Then I shall do it myself. As it is, I have a television. I shall go home and watch it. After I hear the truth revealed, then I shall, as I say, finally be able to go to sleep."

"Hope, if…"

But Hope Reddington had heard and said enough.

She rose, walked quickly to the door, turned, and said, "Please, the two of you— tell the truth."

And she left.

For a time they simply stared at each other.

"Edie, we have to tell Herndon about this. We have to…"

But Edie simply shook her head, took her phone from her purse, began punching a number into it, and said harshly:

"There's only one thing we really have to do; and we really have to do it right now."

"What's that?"

She did not answer but spoke into the phone:

"Jackson? Jackson Bennett? Hi. Edie Towler. We've got a situation here at the hospital. No, there have been no shootings, and Cory Morgan, if it's really him, still hasn't been found. Nothing too much has happened since you left, in fact. And yet—well, something very important may have happened. I'm sorry it's late, but we really do need to talk to you. Yes. Yes, she's been moved to a different room, one in intensive care. No she's fine, it's just…well, security is better here. They'll tell you the room number at the desk when you arrive. I'll call and tell them to let you through and into the hospital. All right. We'll see you in a few minutes."

She pressed on the screen and the phone went dark.

"I feel a great need," she said quietly, "for a cigarette."

"I didn't know you smoked, Edie."

"I don't. Never have. Always regretted that."

"We have to tell them, don't we?"

"Tell who?"

"Herndon."

"Tell him what?"

"Hope's story."

"It's just that—a story."

"You don't believe her?"

"Hope's eighty-six years old."

"Yes and I'm seventy. That doesn't mean I'm necessarily insane."

"I didn't say she was insane."

"It's what you're implying."

A shake of the head.

"I'm not implying anything. I'm just saying that Hope has lived alone for a long time now, a great many years. Some terrible things have happened in her life, and she's gone through a great deal of pain."

"You think that's somehow 'warped' her?"

"I think that before this story—and it really does seem incredible—before it comes out, either by us or by Hope—it might be prudent to have her examined by a psychologist."

"So you do think she's crazy?"

"I think she's heard about some shocking things that have happened here. She may have had some fantasies about things that may or may not have happened in her past. She may be connecting all the dots in the wrong way. Her husband died tragically. Her daughter and son-in-law died tragically. It's her fault, God is punishing her. Why would God be punishing her? Cory Morgan! Maybe she did something to Cory Morgan or his family. Maybe this is God's vengeance. Maybe...I don't know. Maybe we just wait for a little."

And they did.

For five minutes.

Ten.

Finally, the room phone buzzed. Nina picked it up and said:

"Is it Jackson Bennett? All right, send him in."

And within minutes he was in the room with them, shaking his head:

"Wow, it's quite a scene out there. Looks like they're shooting a movie."

"What's happening?" asked Edie. "It's like a womb in here, and we can't see anything."

"Helicopters and searchlights are what's happening. The state police are arriving."

"My God. Just what we need."

Silence for a time, then:

"Thank you," said Nina as he was seating himself, "for taking Furl in, Jackson."

He smiled.

"Furl and I are old friends. What happened to him?"

"Story for another time."

"All right—whenever you want to tell me."

"Jackson," said Edie, "I have some tough questions."

"Legal questions?"

"Yes."

"Then shoot."

"All right, here's the first one. If a man is in prison, can he bring a lawsuit against another party?"

Jackson smiled, "Edie that's one of the great myths surrounding the legal profession, and I've got no idea how it could have started."

"What myth?"

"That a convicted felon cannot sue. That's simply absurd—of course he can."

She was silent for a time and then continued:

"All right. Then, here's a hypothetical case: you know the fifty thousand dollars Harrison Morgan was accused of stealing?"

"Yes."

"Suppose just for a moment—that someone else in Bay St. Lucy did actually steal that money."

His eyes narrowed and he leaned forward in his chair.

"What are you talking about?"

"I'm talking about a supposition."

"That someone else stole the money?"

"Yes."

"But as far as I'm told, the case was iron clad."

"And it probably *was* iron clad. Again, I'm just playing here."

"And a strange game it is."

He looked at Nina and then at Edie, finally saying:

"Do the two of you know something?"

"If we did," asked Edie, "would we be compelled to tell you?"

A shake of his head.

"No, you would not."

"But if you knew something, as an officer of the court, then *you* would be compelled to tell it?"

"Absolutely."

"And what you're telling us is, that if someone other than Harrison Morgan stole that money all those years ago, and now admitted it, then Mr. Cory Morgan, even though he had recently committed cold blooded murder, would have a viable lawsuit against that person."

"You mean the person who, by committing the crime of theft, had directly caused the suicide of an innocent person and ruined the life of Cory Morgan himself as well as his mother? You're asking me if he would have a lawsuit against that person?"

"Yes."

"Well then the answer is this: not only would he have a billion dollar wrongful death lawsuit against that person—who, by the way, would still be eligible to be tried for embezzlement himself—or herself—but he would also have grounds, if the books could be examined and malfeasance proved on the part of the auditors who had accused him in the first place, against that particular firm of auditors, and against the hospital itself. And by the way, I would *love* to be the attorney representing Mr. Morgan in this case—no matter what crimes he had committed in his life."

Silence for a time.

Or rather, near silence.

Nina thought she could hear the sound of helicopter rotor blades, and the muted blare of bullhorns.

"Thank you, Jackson," said Edie.

"My pleasure. But if I can advise you, if either of the two of you know something that is genuinely relevant to this matter…"

"We understand. Thank you again, Jackson. It was very good of you to come."

He took this, correctly, as an invitation to go, and he did.

Leaving them alone.

Except for, of course, the thousand or so paramilitary police troops that were now spreading out over the hospital grounds as though they were Anzio Beachhead.

"My God," whispered Nina after a time.

"Now do you want a cigarette?"

"I see your point."

"Nina, this is a terrible situation. We thought we were up against a psychotic killer."

"Which we still are."

"But we're also up against an impossible choice here."

"I'm still not sure we have a choice. If we don't make this admission on behalf of Hope Reddington, she's going to do it herself."

"Maybe."

"I don't see any 'maybe' about it. Edie, the woman seems completely resolved."

"Maybe we can unresolve her."

"And we would do that why?"

Edie shook her head and leaned forward, "Nina, this admission would devastate Helen and John. Three people close to Hope—her husband, her daughter and her son in law—have already suffered tragedies. Now, if she goes through with this, the cyclical curse would just continue."

"The House of Atreus."

"Pardon?"

"It's just a literature thing. I'm always talking about such stuff, the schoolteacher in me coming out. Paris runs off with Helen, Menelaus' wife. The Greeks, led by Agamemnon, Menelaus' brother, go kill Trojans and there's war for seven years. Agamemnon comes home from the wars with a mistress, and his wife Clytemnestra slaughters him in his bath. Her son and daughter, Orestes and Electra, murder her. The Furies, the dogs of guilt, pursue and torment them the way they must have been torturing Hope all these years. Finally, a god steps in and says, 'That's it!' Stop! No more vengeance disguised as justice. You have to make an end to it!"

"That's what I'm saying, Nina. Maybe we need—maybe Bay St. Lucy needs—some god to step in and say 'stop.'"

"But doesn't Cory Morgan deserve to have his father's name cleared, Edie?"

"No one even remembers his father. And if you want to get your family's name cleared, committing murder is not the way to do it."

"We don't know he's committed murder."

"We know somebody handcuffed that body to the back seat of and then blew up the car. And it looks as though that same person is about to start killing people in this hospital. We know someone, somehow, filled an IV bag with an opioid solution, which would have killed you but for the grace of God and Lalima Singh. You think those crimes were justified, no matter what happened years ago?"

Nina could only shake her head.

She knew nothing to say.

But Edie continued, "And it gets worse, don't you see? Yes, the admission would be devastating to John and Helen. Two lives at least—and a third if we count Cory himself—ruined because of a crime committed by Helen's father, whom she has looked upon for all these years as something of a saint. I don't know how you get over that. But it goes beyond that. Nina, this is a terrible indictment of the entire community. If what Hope says is true, then it's not just Marshall Reddington who wronged the Morgans. It's Bay St. Lucy. Francine Morgan came to the hospital and threw herself in front of everyone for understanding, for mercy. She got nothing, a cold shoulder. You know that saying. 'It takes a village to raise a child?' Well, in this case it took a village to destroy one. And his family."

"All right, Edie. All right, Mayor Towler. So what do you think we should do?"

Edie merely pursed her lips and shook her head:

"I'm going to make an admission to you. And no matter what happens to Cory Morgan, you're never to tell a soul that I said this to you."

"All right."

"I have your word?"

"You have my word."

"Well, as I see it, two things can happen in the next few hours to Cory Morgan."

"And those things are?"

"There are now a million or so highly trained police out there, and very soon in here. Not Moon's local people, but the best in the state. They're either going to catch Cory Morgan—and when they do they're going to cart him away immediately and not listen to any story about what may or may not have happened to his father—"

"Or?"

"Or they're going to kill him."

Nina could feel her mouth drop open, and her next words came out of it as from an automaton:

"Edie, are you saying that's what you want?"

"I don't know. I don't know what I want. I'm just saying that, with Cory Morgan dead, and Hope staying quiet about the theft—the whole thing goes away."

But Nina could only shake her head:

"No, it doesn't go away. It's a sin, Edie, a vicious ugly sin that's just as much a part of the heart of this community as the hospital is the heart of this community. If you and I simply cover this thing up— and somehow persuade Hope to do so—could you ever look on Bay St. Lucy in the same way again?"

There was silence for a time; then Edie rose, took three quick steps toward the door and said quietly, "I have to go."

"Where are you going?"

"I don't know. I have to think. I'll be back. I just—I have to think. Nina—"

"Yes?"

"Please don't do anything rash while I'm gone."

"Like calling Chip Herndon?"

"Like calling Chip Herndon. Or re-calling Jackson Bennett. Don't do either of those things. Maybe we do have to do as Hope says. Maybe we have to give out the story. But let's think it through well. Very very well. Because if we do, Bay St. Lucy will never be the same again. I have to go now."

And she left.

Nina could only watch the door close.

Finally, she whispered to the empty room, "Jane, where are you? Jane Austen, if ever I needed you..."

The words formulated themselves in her mind—

'A mind lively and at ease can do with seeing nothing, and can see nothing that does not answer.'

—then the words dissolved into thin air.

Because they had no meaning in this situation, no relevance at all.

This was not a question of some small detail that had been overlooked and, once uncovered, would reveal THE TRUTH.

No, in this case THE TRUTH stood before her in the middle of the room, massive and hideous.

The question was simply what to do about it.

"Frank?"

But Frank did not appear.

And THE TRUTH remained precisely where it was.

CHAPTER SIXTEEN: THE BOY WITH RED HAIR
9:50 P.M.

Nina could hear ever so faintly the tolling of bells in
Bay St. Lucy's Catholic Church.

She could have been a mouse, a church mouse, in
any of the town's churches, she found herself thinking.
Still, still, just listening and watching.

Would church be the same anymore?

The Methodist Church, every Sunday, services at ten
A.M., she and Frank, never missing, third pew from the
back. Opening hymn, perhaps written by Fanny Crosby,
'Everyone please stand!,' and she mouthing the words
because she could not sing, Frank with his reedy tenor
voice, a high harmony seeping out.

"For we are dwelling in Beulah Land!"

"What a fellowship what a joy divine!"

and of course:

"Bless be the tie that binds, our hearts in Christian
love."

Christian love, all of us bound together.

In a community.

Supporting each other.

Would church ever be the same?

Would her life be the same?

She had, for so long, been Nina the good, Nina the
wise. The best principal in the history of Bay St. Lucy
High School. Whatever problem had come up—Bridget
O'Leary's pregnancy, whatever problem—she had,
even if unable to solve it, at least been a comforting
presence. And in the past years, the Lissie Movement,

the horrible discovery of Edgar Martinez' body and subsequent events unfolding on board The Aquatica—somehow she had been the moral center of the community.

With prayer and thought, she had known what to do.

And now she simply did not.

And now she simply...

These reveries were interrupted by a clattering noise outside the room, a muffled banging, the door opening, and two figures, Michael Yancy and the same Bridget O'Leary she had just been thinking of, pushing before them a small metal cart with a portable television set on top of it.

"Still awake?" asked Bridget.

Still awake. What a question.

"Yes, I'm awake. Dr. Singh gave me a mild sedative, and I may have dozed for a second or so—but—"

"But you had a visitor, we hear."

"Yes. Hope Reddington was just here."

"I remember the Reddingtons. I hadn't seen her since I got back to Bay St. Lucy."

"Well, she's in her eighties. She doesn't get out too much."

"I'm surprised she came tonight. So late and with this weather. Somehow she convinced Dr. Singh to let her come up. It must have been important."

It must have been important.

"It was to her."

"Probably just wanted to tell you how much you mean to her."

Actually she wanted to tell me her husband stole fifty thousand dollars and destroyed a family.

"Yes. That was it. How much she meant to me."

Yancy stepped around the cart and prepared to turn on the television set.

"How are you doing, Ms.—how are you doing, Nina?"

"I'm good, Michael," she lied. "Thank you for going to my house and checking on Furl."

"My pleasure. I heard he showed up here at the hospital."

"Yes, he's fine."

"I'm so glad to hear that. Anyway, Moon asked me to come up and check on you."

"You can tell Moon I'm okay."

"I will."

"What's the television for?"

Bridget:

"Well, you'll notice there aren't any in the E.R. rooms."

"I can understand why there aren't."

"Of course. But apparently another news story is about to break."

"Herndon?"

"That's the word. The T.V. people called the hospital to warn us about it. They've apparently learned some 'breaking news from the state police. When Dr. Singh got wind of it, she asked me to bring a T.V. set in. She's given up any hope of your sleeping, at least for some time. She told me it's important for you to know what everybody else does, and when."

"That's nice of her. It's good to be 'in the know.'"

Except it isn't.

It stinks.

She thought of Hope Reddington, who by now would just be getting home. And perhaps turning on her television set.

Expecting to see Nina and Edie revealing her secret?

What would she do when no such secret was revealed?

Call Chip Herndon herself, as she had threatened to do?

And if she did so, would…

But this train of thought was derailed by the click of the *on* button and the now all too familiar face of Chip Herndon in the foreground, the military-style preparations of state police on the hospital yard in the background.

"Hello, Bay St. Lucy! This is Chip Herndon with yet more to report on what is becoming an ever more astonishing story, and one whose center continues to be the city hospital. As you can see behind me, the Mississippi State Police Department is now taking over the investigation, searching for a young man who may have committed one murder tonight, and who seems to be threatening more violence. The young man, judging from a note that he had apparently written, is attempting to clear the name of his father, who was convicted of embezzling fifty thousand dollars from the Bay St. Lucy Hospital fund. That money was never found. Mr. Morgan committed suicide before being taken away, and his wife and thirteen-year-old son—who was indeed named Cory—simply disappeared. Authorities in Bay St. Lucy simply decided to drop the matter, finding it highly unlikely that the missing fifty thousand dollars could be recovered by putting the wife and son under further scrutiny."

Herndon took a deep breath and then continued:

"But as I told you earlier, we have breaking news. The computerized tracking system of the state police force has determined that Francine Morgan passed away one week ago in Ruston, Louisiana, after a year-long battle with lung cancer. They also learned that she had been living with her son, Cory, now twenty three years old and employed as a nurse's aide at Ruston

Memorial Hospital. Efforts to contact young Robinson at his home have so far failed."

"Because," Nina found herself whispering, "he's not at his home. He's here."

"What did you say?" asked Bridget.

"Nothing," replied Nina, "that we don't already know."

And she did know.

She knew about Hope, and now she knew about Cory.

There was nothing she could prove, nothing she could even back up by the most sophisticated literary analysis or praying to the God of Jane Austen.

But she knew it. As a woman she knew it. She had never been a mother, but if she had, her knowledge would even be more rock solid.

Francine Morgan had left Bay St. Lucy hating the town and everyone in it. This hatred had been shared by her young son, and had festered within him during his teenage years. He had, at some point, almost certainly vowed to take revenge.

Which his mother had prevented him from doing.

Having lost a husband, she had no desire to lose a son.

Vengeance was thus not taken.

But now she was dead.

And Cory was here.

The screen changed and flashed a deep red.

"This," Chip Herndon was saying, "is Cory Morgan."

The face of any young man in his early twenties, marked by one unmistakable difference. From this face shot out flaming ringlets of bright red hair.

And Nina continued to whisper to herself, "How could he have been here and not been seen?"

So many things were making sense to her now.

But where was this young man?

The broadcast droned on for a time, with Nina's thoughts racing this way and that. Finally it ended, Bridget looked at her ankle and did a blood pressure check.

Same old same old.

Finally she was left in the room with Michael Yancy, who turned off the television set, saying as he did so:

"There will be more broadcasts. Might as well leave the set here."

"Yes. I guess so."

More broadcasts.

Would she and Edie be featured on the next one?

Or would Hope?

"I guess that explains one thing," Michael was saying.

"What?"

"The IV bag with the opioid solution. He works in a hospital. He knows his way around in one."

Nina nodded:

"Yes, it follows."

"Nina…"

She could sense that he wanted to say something to her and that the something was more complex, more difficult, than 'I'm glad your ankle is doing okay.'"

"What is it, Michael?"

He sat down, then shook his head and said, quietly:

"It's just a feeling I had. A crazy feeling. But strong. And I can't get rid of it."

"What kind of feeling?"

Fingers interlaced, he threw back his head and looked up at the ceiling:

"I first got it when I was over at your house. When I was walking up the outside stairs and then when I was standing in your living room."

"Go on."

"I knew he wasn't there, this guy. But I knew he had been on those stairs, had been in that room."

"How did you know?"

A shake of the head.

"Can't tell. I just did. But I knew it. For absolute certain I knew it. And I knew something else too, Nina. For just as certain."

"What do you know, Michael?"

He looked straight at her, saying, "I will meet this man. I will meet him tonight. And either I will kill him. Or he will kill me."

Nina knew nothing to say to this.

She was attempting to formulate a reply when Moon Rivard stuck his head in the door and said:

"I'm sorry to bother you Ms. Nina—but it looks like it can't be helped."

"What is it, Moon?"

"The man says he has to talk to you. And he's my boss. I guess he's the boss of all of us."

"Who is this man?"

"His name is Hall. He's a captain in The Mississippi State Police Department. He's heading the investigation now."

She sighed and said quietly:

"All right, Moon. Send him in."

But it was not necessary to give her permission.

The large-boned man pushing his way through the doorway at that instant did not need it.

CHAPTER SEVENTEEN: CAPTAIN THOMAS HALL
10:00 P.M.

Captain Thomas Hall was a man of acute angles. There were no soft curves about his body or his personality. A line drawn straight down the bridge of his nose would have crossed a line tracing his lantern jaw at precisely sixty-three degrees.

Such lines covered his body and his being.

They defined him.

When he walked into Nina's room and sat down, two of his paramilitary-looking officers standing watch over him as though offering protection from the non-linear world, Moon Rivard trailing behind, Michael Yancy shoved aside like an unwanted pet of some species—when he sat in this precise and mathematical way, Nina found herself wondering if he were a human being or a set of drawings in an engineering textbook.

"You are Ms. Bannister, I believe?"

"Yes."

"Ms. Nina Bannister?"

"Yes."

"Ma'am, my name is Captain Thomas Hall. I'm headquartered in Jackson. As you probably know by now, I and a number of my men are taking over this investigation."

"I am aware of that."

"My office has now had some time to do our investigative work. You probably heard the news broadcast giving out what we have learned about the Morgan family."

Yes, I did hear it."

"Then I want to make one thing clear at the outset, Ms. Bannister: and that is, we have no idea of the whereabouts of Mr. Cory Morgan. We know that his mother died approximately a week ago. We know his address; we know that he has not been at that address for the last few days, or possibly since the death of his mother."

"I know all of those things. We have a hard working group of newsmen here in Bay St. Lucy."

Captain Hall nodded and said:

"My office has no secrets from the press, and we like to work with them whenever we can. Apparently the local police force was less than forthcoming about several features of this case early on. That's unfortunate. It only led to the propagation of rumors and the stoking of potential panic in the town."

This criticism was clearly aimed at Moon, but he remained expressionless in the room's far corner, and Hall did not look at him.

"At any rate, authorities around the state are now aware of this—well let's just call it a 'situation.' The head of the Mississippi State Police is aware of it; the governor is aware of it."

"That's comforting," she said, wondering if the man before her understood sarcasm.

If he did, his next comments gave no hint of the fact.

"The upshot of it all is this: if this young man is here in the hospital, or anywhere else, we need to find him immediately, apprehend him, learn if he is responsible for a crime or crimes, and, if this is the case, put him in custody."

Or kill him, she found herself thinking.

"My own first job though is to speak with you. I hope you're feeling well enough to make this possible."

"I'm fine. I'm really just here for observation. Dr. Singh told me I should be going home tomorrow."

"Excellent. So let us get into the core of this matter."

"I'm ready."

"You received a message that allegedly had been written by Cory Morgan."

"I received it two hours ago approximately. It said my job was to clear the name of his father. If I didn't, he would begin killing people."

"And since that time all contacts with this Mr. Morgan have been through you."

"That is correct."

"You found the first message just before the car exploded downstairs?"

"Yes, a few minutes before."

"I see. Now I have had a chance to do some research on this Morgan trial. Talk to some people. You had been supportive of the Morgans ten years ago when this crime took place."

"Yes. I guess I was one of the few people who actually did try to help them. I was high school principal at the time. Francine Morgan taught English."

"Your thinking then is that Cory trusts you and wants to work through you in clearing the name of his father."

"That would seem to make sense."

"All right then. That all seems clear up to now. So I must ask you point blank: Ms. Bannister, do you know anything about this matter that you aren't telling us? Anything that I should definitely know?"

And there it was.

No one in the room—the other officers, Yancy, Moon—moved, or, seemingly, even breathed.

It was not a hospital room. It was the still life painting of a hospital room.

Did she know anything that the rest of them needed to know?

Well, yes, come to think of it, she did. She knew that Hope Reddington's husband had actually taken the fifty thousand dollars to pay gambling debts, and that the whole trial of Harrison Morgan had been a sham, completely manipulated by Homer Baron Robinson for the purpose of paying of New Orleans gamblers.

She also suspected that Cory Morgan had been stopped by his mother from seeking revenge on Bay St. Lucy and on its hospital in particular.

But Francine Morgan was dead now; any promises he might have made to her were null and void.

These things she knew. And they helped her not one bit. They were simply facts, lying around the hospital like so many tinker toys. The question went beyond facts. The question was, what should she do? Tell the truth of course. That's what Nina Bannister had always been taught to do.

But if she did it in this case, the Reddingtons would be disgraced. Helen and John would never get over it. Nor would Bay St. Lucy. The town, its citizens, and, in particular, the hospital would be liable to a million dollar lawsuit, a suit brought by someone who might well be sitting on—if the person handcuffed in the exploding car had really been murdered—death row.

What would be the good of all that?

If she did not tell, though, then Hope had promised to do so herself.

But she could be talked out of doing so, could she not?

She, Nina, and Edie Towler might be able to reason with her.

These were the things that flashed through her mind.

"Ms. Bannister? Did you understand my question?"

Of course she understood the question. It was simply the answer that was giving her trouble. Tell the truth, Nina. Tell the truth.

And so thinking—she lied.

"There's nothing more I can add. Nothing you don't already know. This Mr. Morgan—or someone with a raspy and disguised voice claiming to be Mr. Morgan—called Edie Towler about an hour ago and said that the body was that of Edie's father. It wasn't."

"I've been apprised of that."

"Someone apparently went to my house, also about an hour ago, took my cat, called me to try to make me think the cat had been harmed, and brought the cat here to the hospital."

"Again—these are all things I knew. You've got nothing else?"

She lied again, "No."

Causing Captain Hall to take a deep breath before continuing:

"Then it's going to be my duty, Ms. Bannister, to put some hard questions to you. Some very hard questions."

What's he getting at? Nina found herself thinking.

"It's been my experience that people—sometimes, especially, older people, people who live alone—will imagine the existence of a crime. Will fabricate it completely in their minds, make themselves somehow the center of it. They are, in their own minds, either the victims of the crime or even the culprits, the guilty parties."

My God, she thought.

He knows about Hope.

Somehow Hope has contacted him.

Why, Hope?

Why didn't you wait, like Edie advised you to do?

Her voice stammered out into the room, dry and shaky:

"Do you have such a person in mind?"

"I do have such a person in mind, Ms. Bannister. And I suspect that you do, too."

All right, Nina. There's no chance to cover up Hope's confession now. Just say it:

"Yes, I'll admit it. You just have to see that…"

"You wrote that message, didn't you, Ms. Bannister?"

It took a moment for this question to sink in.

"What?"

Still sinking in.

Still sinking.

Only one question remained appropriate, "What?"

The room collapsed inward, with Moon and Yancy being sucked in toward the captain, amazed expressions on each of their faces.

"You—you think that I—you think—"

"I think the whole Cory Morgan business may be coming from this hospital bed."

There were cries of disbelief coming from Moon and Michael Yancy.

Nina lay perfectly still, as though struck by lightning.

But the captain, whose dark brown uniform was now making him look like a tree with a wrinkled face on top of it, merely half smiled and calmly continued, "It's all right. I understand the forces that make people do these things. But you yourself have to understand now—it's time to end this. Now."

"End what?"

The tree sighed.

"You are a woman of a certain age. You live alone. We've been in town for a little more than an hour now, and my men have been able to contact a good many of your friends."

It was as though someone else was speaking, formulating Nina-like words that came out of a Nina-like mouth, "Which friends?"

"That really doesn't matter now, does it?"

"Of course it does! You've been going around my town talking with my friends behind my back?"

"Do you really think it's *your* town, ma'am?"

"Not in the sense that I own it, but it's just—"

"Just that you like to feel as though you're the center of it, right? You like to feel as though things revolve around you. You enjoy, in short, getting attention."

"That's the most…"

"But you hadn't been getting attention in the last few weeks, had you? Several people close to you told us that you hadn't really been 'yourself.'"

"Who said that about me?"

"All I can say is that we had it from more than one source."

"All right I was a bit blue. But that doesn't mean I would make up this whole nightmare that's happening. A car really did explode, you know! A body— somebody's—is really lying over there at the morgue!"

"And that went along well with the 'threat message' game you had concocted, didn't it?"

"The what?"

"The message game!"

"That's the most absurd thing I've ever heard!"

"No. The most absurd thing anyone has ever heard is that a young man—hardly more than a boy, really—a young man with flaming red hair could blow up a car with a human being in it, then go and come through the halls of this hospital, writing notes and making strange phone calls, breaking into your house, playing tricks on the mayor concerning her father—and never be seen or noticed by anyone at all—especially during the night shift in a relatively small hospital, where all the doctors, orderlies and nurses all know each other well, and would recognize immediately any stranger who might be lurking around. *That* is an absurd thing—in fact it's completely absurd!"

She knew nothing to say.

Only one thought formulated itself in her mind:

This idiot had no notion of Hope Reddington.

That secret was still safe.

But as for her—she did not feel so safe.

What were they going to do, put her away?

Hall continued, "What is not absurd is that no one has had any contact with the alleged Cory Robinson except through you. Now think: the young man's mother did in fact die of cancer in Ruston, Louisiana, approximately a week ago. You might well have heard of that. How I'm not sure but since she was an ex-resident of the town—well, let's say you somehow learned of it. You were sympathetic with young Robinson during his father's ordeal. Hearing about his mother, feeling sorry for him after all these years, and battling depression yourself—"

"I wasn't 'battling depression.'"

"That's not the way we hear it."

"What you're hearing is complete garbage!"

"You're friends are lying about you?"

"They're not my...I mean..."

"They aren't really your friends? You don't have any friends, is that what you're saying?"

"This is the most bizarre..."

"Look—Nina. Your name is Nina, isn't it?"

"Yes."

"May I call you Nina?"

"No."

"All right then, we can make it difficult. I'm not saying you're completely fabricating all of this simply to get attention. I am saying that your trip to the emergency room, the medications prescribed to you, the experience of having to be in the hospital…"

"You're saying I'm crazy?"

"I'm saying that, at least in your mind, Cory Robinson may really have returned to Bay St. Lucy."

"So you *are* saying I'm crazy!"

"I'm raising the possibility that you may be hallucinating."

"And that I wrote a threatening note without knowing it?"

"You felt that Cory Robinson was acting through you. And when the note had the effect that it did have—and the phone calls too—why you were the center of attention again. Just as you wanted."

"That's the most absurd thing I've ever heard in my life! And what about the IV? Someone tried to inject Gray Death into me!"

"Yeah, we've also heard about that. And you think this Cory Morgan was responsible? A kid with a shock of red hair who's been floating around here like a ghost, nobody seeing him. This kid somehow was able to break into the supply room and switch out IV bags in one of the most secure areas of this hospital?"

"All right I know it seems hard to believe."

"It seems impossible to believe."

"Then how did the opioid get into the bag?"

"How do you think it did? I'll tell you: sheer incompetence. That or panic."

"What are you talking about?"

"I'm talking about the fact that everyone around here seems to have been running around like chickens with their heads cut off for the past few hours, or at least ever since that car blew up. I'm amazed anybody got the right medicine, and I'm amazed that somebody hasn't been poisoned for real. There is, as I understand it, only one real doctor on call here at the moment. And she's not even a real American doctor. Where did she go to school, India or someplace like that?"

"So now you're insulting Dr. Singh?"

"I'm just stating facts."

Moon, unable to restrain himself any longer, stepped forward and said, almost shouting:

"I've heard enough of this, Hall!"

"It's Captain Hall to you."

"When you act like an officer, damn it, I'll treat you like an officer!"

"That's enough! You're off this case! So are your men! And you've all been off it since my people arrived half an hour ago. And as for incompetence—why this whole thing is a mess. You have, as far as I can tell, done nothing but commit one blunder after another. Now you've got the whole town chasing an imaginary 'psycho killer' when the cause of the whole panic is lying right here in front of you."

"You can't talk about Ms. Bannister like that!" shouted Michael Yancy, taking a step toward the captain.

His pathway was blocked by one of the state policemen, but he too was now almost to the point of shouting, "She's obviously one of the most respected women in Bay St. Lucy! You ought to apologize to her! Right now!"

But Captain Hall merely continued to shake his head, looking not at Yancy but at Moon, and saying, "Rivard, you need to get your people away from this hospital. And I mean *right now*! Amateur hour is over. This 'officer'—Yancy or whatever his name is—is not much more than a child, and it's inexcusable to let him run around here armed."

Now to Michael:

"Son you need to go back home tonight before you hurt somebody."

And that, Nina found herself thinking, was going to happen soon.

There were five armed people in the room, three of them red-faced and shouting, the other two standing with their hands solemnly and terrifyingly resting on their revolvers.

And while all of this drama was ongoing, Nina found herself unable to avoid the question that kept inserting itself into her mind:

Was she going crazy?

Three hours ago she had looked down at what should have been an ankle—*her* ankle—and seen a monstrous thing, a swollen mass of flesh that was not Nina Bannister nor any part of her.

This because of a blood clot.

But could the same blood clot have done something to her brain? Several types of medication had been pumped into her during the past two hours. Perhaps she *was* hallucinating.

At any rate, she could not remain unaware of the strange irony underlying events as they were unfolding. Edie was suggesting that Hope, elderly, might have fantasized a crime; now Hall was suggesting that Nina—also elderly, no denying it—could have fantasized a killer.

And while these thoughts pushed their way into her brain, normal or addled, whichever it might have been—the shouting in the room continued—Hall took a menacing step toward Moon and barked, "I'm going to say this one more time, 'Officer' Rivard! You get out of here, and you get your men out of here, and I mean quick. I'm going to be holding a news conference downstairs, just outside of the main entrance to the ER.

I want it to be right where the other conferences took place. And I'm going to try—try mind you—to assure folks in this town that there is no psychotic killer roaming the halls of this hospital or the streets of this town."

"But you don't know that, dammit! Somebody sure as hell called Mayor Towler and told her that her father was burned in that car! Also, somebody went over to Ms. Nina's house, got her cat, and brought him here to the hospital!"

"Yes, we're aware of those things. So first, the call. Were you here in the room with Ms. Bannister when it was made?"

"No, but…"

"Was anybody with her?"

"I don't know that…but…"

"So *she* could have made the call. Just like she could have made any calls and written any of the letters that are causing this stir. As for the cat, she could have brought it over with her when she checked in. Ms. Bannister?"

Nina felt as though she had been watching a low budget movie.

But now she realized she was being called back to reality.

Or that she was being pulled farther into the film.

Who knew?

At any rate, she felt compelled to answer.

"Yes?"

Hall now seemed to be towering over her.

"Ms. Bannister, I'm going to recommend that you undergo a psychiatric examination as soon as possible, preferably tomorrow morning. If you refuse, I have the power to force you to do so by naming you as a 'person of interest' in the events of this evening."

She was about to answer—although she had no idea when she took a deep breath and prepared to listen to herself exactly what her answer would be—when Moon spoke for her, saying:

"That kind of a test would be an insult to Ms. Nina."

"And your precious 'Ms. Nina' has been insulting your city police force as well as your entire hospital for the last three hours. Now I've told you once and I'll tell you again: stand down. In ten minutes I'm going to tell the city as well as the state of Mississippi that you've been relieved. I don't want to see any of your people around here when I do that."

So saying, he left, taking his soldiers with him.

This left Moon, Michael Yancy, and Nina in the room

It was Yancy who spoke up first.

"So what do I do?"

Moon merely shook his head and growled.

"Go back to the station. They see you around here— hell, son, they could arrest you."

"Does he have the power to do that? Where does he get the authority to order us around like that?"

"He gets it from the governor. And he's got all the power he wants."

Yancy nodded, took two steps toward the door, then turned back and spoke to Nina:

"You shouldn't worry, ma'am."

"Nina."

"Sorry. Nina."

"I've already been called everything but 'senile.' Don't *ma'am* me."

"Like I say, I'm sorry. But you really shouldn't worry. You didn't write the note or make the calls. You didn't do any of those things. We all know that."

"Thank you, Michael. Now you better do what Moon says, so that you don't get arrested."

"All right. I'm gone then."

And he too left the room.

Nina spoke to Moon:

"Well, I guess the two of us got put in our place."

"Yes. Guess we did."

"In a way I hope he's right. That would mean no Cory Morgan in the halls, and no more killings to come tonight."

"Yes. That's the truth. And now that I look close at it, he is right about one thing. He's right about me. I sure ain't done too good. Everyone's in a panic. Investigation going to be better off without me. He's sure right about that."

"No, he isn't."

"Good of you to say that."

"So what are you going to do now, Moon?"

A shrug:

"What I'm ordered to do. Go back to the station. Talk to my men. I got to let all of them know this ain't their fault. Before I do that though I'd kind of like to listen to this conference he's done set up for himself."

"I would too."

"You sure?"

"Yes. If he's going to blame the whole thing on me, I want to know it. The television they brought in for me is still workable I guess. Let's turn it on."

They did.

Thank heaven, an old black and white movie.

Would that it could keep running all night.

It did not, of course, and after five minutes the scene changed.

The first thing Nina noticed about the front of the hospital was that it looked like yet another movie.

A war movie.

Military style vehicles were now parked where normal cars and trucks had been parked an hour ago.

Spotlights were everywhere.

In the center of one of the largest spotlights, a podium had been built.

Captain Hall stood behind it, flanked by several town notables, among them Edie Towler.

"Are you going to interrupt his speech and tell them about Hope?" Nina whispered to the screen.

"Or are you going to let him tell the whole town that Nina Bannister has lost her mind?"

Moon leaned toward her:

"What did you say, Ms. Bannister?"

"Nothing. I just…"

She was interrupted by the first of Hall's remarks, "Good evening, Bay St. Lucy, and good evening Mississippi. My name is Captain Thomas Hall. I'm an officer in the Mississippi State Police Force. I want to begin by assuring you that many of the things you have heard tonight are no more than rumors. I also want to make clear the fact that…"

Nina attempted to concentrate on what he was saying, but she was distracted by Moon, who leaned toward the screen, and rumbled, "He's got all his men down there."

And it was true. There were at least a dozen of them, at attention, lined in three rows.

"Is that bad, Moon?"

"Wouldn't normally be. Show of force. Make the town think everything's gonna be okay It's just that…"

"That what?"

"My own men are headed back to headquarters. If his are all down there behind him, then…"

He did not finish the sentence.

Hall continued, "It is now our considered opinion that we have been victimized by a kind of hoax. Yes, there was earlier in the evening a tragic car explosion, which claimed a life. But there is no psychotic killer roaming the halls of the hospital. There is no..."

At that moment there came a small 'crack.'

Thomas Hall sank to his knees, then pitched forward on the platform.

"What happened?" gasped Nina.

Moon, already on his feet and heading toward the door, shouted back over his shoulder:

"The man's been shot."

CHAPTER SEVENTEEN: REQUIEM
10:30 P.M.

Moon had almost hurtled through the doorway when his two way radio began to squawk. He ripped it off his black leather belt as though it were a handgun and barked into it, "Yeah, whoever you are be damned quick; we've got an emergency going on down below—a man's been shot!"

Nina could recognize the voice emerging from the speaker as that of Michael Yancy, almost in panic:

"I got him!"

Moon scowled and appeared ready to eat the shining metal object he was holding up to his mouth.

"What? Is this Yancy?"

"It's Yancy! I got him, boss!"

She heard labored heavy breathing as though the speaker were running hard. There were also pounding sounds made by boots on metallic stairs.

"What are you talking about, kid?"

"I'm on the back stairway leading down to Exit 4 in the back of the building!"

"So what the hell's going on?"

"Cory Morgan's just run out of the building, red hair and all! He's carrying a rifle—I don't know what he did with it."

"What he did with it is, he shot Hall!"

"Oh my God!"

"Who else is down there with you, Yancy?"

"Nobody! The whole building's deserted down here. Where are all the cops?"

"I had to pull our people out—Hall was so certain we were daydreaming that he had his men out standing in formation, listening to his damn speech!"

"Okay, I got it. Hold on!"

More labored breathing, more boot pounding.

She could hear the sounds of sirens filtering through the speaker and through the thick walls insulating her room.

After some seconds:

"I'm outside now. There he is! He's got a car and he's pulling out through the rear exit of the parking lot! Nobody around to stop him!"

"Wait for back up, Yancy!"

"I can't or I'll lose him. There's a squad car right on the other side of the street here. I'm using it!"

Moon frowned and growled, his mouth now some distance from the speaker, "Damn kid."

Then, transmitting again:

"I told you to wait for back up!"

"Yeah, I know, but there's nobody coming!"

The sound of a car door slamming, a motor starting.

Tires screeching as the patrol car obviously backed up and spun out into the street.

"He's pulling out onto Breakers Boulevard, Moon. He's driving without lights and he's going damned fast—but I think I can stay with him."

Moon took several deep breaths and glanced at the T.V. screen, which showed a scene of pure chaos.

Then he looked at Nina and said quietly, "I got to let the kid make the chase. This is the only chance we got to catch this psycho—hell, it's the only time we've even had a look at him!"

Then once again into the speaker:

"All right, Yancy—do what you're trained to do. Where are you now?"

"Turning onto Breakers, boss! He's maybe two hundred yards ahead, but there's practically no traffic out here, so I can see him pretty good!"

"Try and keep that spacing. Be sure he keeps moving. If he slows down or stops, don't you approach—remember he's got a rifle of some kind, and he knows how to use it."

"Roger that!"

"Now hold on—I'm gonna patch you through to our state dispatch. Anything you say, all the state police cars will hear—got that?"

"Got it!"

Moon pressed several buttons, then several more buttons.

Finally:

"Right, Yancy—you're on the air with the state police force, at least all of them that are in cars right now. Where are you?"

"We just turned onto Beach Shore Drive!"

"About how far out?"

"Maybe four miles—but we're doing eighty. I don't think any of the state guys are gonna catch up!" Yancy spoke breathlessly.

"All right. You're doing a good job. Just hang in there!"

"I'm hanging. It's just…"

"Just what, Yancy?"

"The sleet's getting harder! I can barely see him now, but…yeah he's turned off the main road and seems to be heading over to the beach."

"How far is the beach from the road you're on now?"

"Can't tell. Maybe a quarter mile."

"And you still can't see him?"

"No. But I'm coming up now on the turn off. Here it is. No name. Just a sand road heading over toward the ocean."

That had to be true, thought Nina. She could hear the roaring of the surf, and in her mind's eye she could imagine black waves pounding the shore, riddled by the sleet.

"You see him?"

"No. I'm pulling up onto the beach now—there are dunes around me. But no car."

"He's got to be there somewhere, dammit!"

"I'm stopping now, and getting out of the squad car. I can hear some patrol cars coming up from Bay St. Lucy."

So could Nina, their thin and tinny whine oozing out of the speaker.

"I'm out of the car now, trying to see if I can find any tracks."

"Don't do that, son."

"He's got to have hidden his car out in these dunes. If I can just find out where he turned off…"

"I'm telling you, Yancy, to stay in the patrol car! Remember: you've got a service revolver; he's got a rifle!"

"I will find this guy. I've got cops arriving now. But we will find him!"

She could hear the sirens louder now in the background, men's voices, shouting, confused.

And then, in the corridor just outside her door, more sirens began to go off.

Lights, harsh and red, went on and off, reminding her of a fire drill.

Or a bomb threat.

She looked at Moon and asked, "What is it, Moon?"

He flipped shut his speaker phone and walked toward the doorway, saying back to her, "Hospital emergency! Someone's being brought in to ER. They only set off this alarm when it's a life threatening emergency. It's got to be Hall!"

And sure enough, a stretcher was being pushed fast in front of nurses and orderlies, who were converging on the room just next to hers.

In the middle of this group she saw Lalima Singh, her face masked as though in preparation for an operation, two nurses helping her pull on long white plastic gloves.

There, at the back of the group, walked Bridget O'Leary.

"Bridget!"

The woman swerved out of the group and, face mask not yet fastened, leaned into the room.

"Bridget!" Nina found herself shouting, "I'm sorry. I know it's an emergency. But what's Captain Hall's condition? We saw it on the television—we saw him pitch forward like he was shot, hit bad. How is he Bridget?"

Bridget O'Leary grasped the door frame with her left hand and said:

"Captain Hall is dead."

Stunned for a second, Nina finally stammered:

"Then who is in there on the stretcher?"

"Hope Reddington. Her daughter Helen is coming up right behind us."

"Helen? Here? And what's happened to Hope?"

"She just tried to commit suicide."

CHAPTER EIGHTEEN: THE DARK EYED HELEN
10:45 P.M.

Helen Giusti, née Helen Reddington, was not large at all. But something about her bearing and grace magnified her. She was much bigger than her size. And her eyes, the darkest most penetrating eyes that Nina had ever seen, sucked the world into them and held it there before mentally digesting it, so that she could decide which parts to keep and which to throw away.

She was dressed in a dark blue pullover sweater and khaki jeans. Casual in short. But Helen was never casual, could never give the appearance of casual, no matter what she chose to wear. No, all of her coloring, all of her subtlety, all of the hauntingly elemental simplicity of her bearing, convinced Nina that, if Bay St. Lucy had ever produced a true princess, then it was the woman who, still sobbing, now threw herself into her arms.

Nina found herself sobbing too, and for a time they simply lay upon the hospital bed, neither one willing to relax her embrace on the other.

While Nina let her mind slip back into the past.

Once again, it was a Friday night, and she and Frank had been invited for dinner at the Reddingtons.

Hope, now fighting for her life in the ER room next door, was all those years ago in the garden with the two men. Nina had come inside the house in order to get something or other from the kitchen. That kind of thing had come to define the nature of the two families' relationship. Hope's kitchen, Nina's kitchen—all one.

She could remember walking carefully, almost reverently, through the dining room with its great oaken table and silver tea service, and through the parlor where sat a golden harp that was played daily by the then young girl who was to become Helen's mother— and finally into the kitchen with its ranges and coolers and cabinets and spices—so that as she walked through these rooms she could swear she was hearing, mixed with her own breathing and the creaking of wooden floorboards, the sound of utter stillness, laughing softly.

And now she was here.

And Hope was…

…well, let that go.

Let it go, and give Helen the chance to cry all she needed to.

And visualize another scene.

The four adults were on the back screened porch now. A white wrought iron table sat directly beneath an overhead fan, which rotated slowly emitting an almost imperceptible creak of gears. Just beyond the far screen wall, almost close enough, it seemed, that she could reach out and touch it, flowed the bayou, making its stately way into the gulf, twenty feet wide here and shining orange brown in the setting sun.

"Oh, Nina…"

And now they were here.

What could she say?

"It's all right, Helen."

Except that it wasn't.

It was nowhere close to all right.

Helen pushed herself back a bit, so that, although still holding Nina in a loose embrace, she could still speak somewhat lucidly.

"It was—I just can't—"

"It's all right. Take your time."

"Well—John's away. He's in Jackson at a convention of veterinarians. I was at home watching television. There was the report, and then another report—all about a shooter loose in Bay St. Lucy…"

"Yes. And apparently they're true, those reports."

They're not Nina Bannister going crazy, despite what 'Captain Hall' might have made himself believe, and tried to force others to believe.

Immediately upon thinking these things she felt guilty.

Whatever else Hall had done, he did not deserve to be shot.

But Helen was continuing, "I thought it would be a good idea to call grandmamma, just to check on her. I even thought I would offer to drive into Bay St. Lucy, or even stay over for the night. That or invite her out to our house. So I called her. But she didn't answer. Nina, this all happened about nine o'clock. Grandmamma never goes to bed before ten. I didn't know where she could be."

I know where she was, thought Nina. She was here at the hospital.

Confessing.

Saying things which, if they get out, may destroy all of your reputations.

"I kept calling. Nine thirty. Ten. I thought she might have fallen asleep on the couch, and that the ringing phone might wake her."

And you were half right, Helen.

She did fall asleep.

Yes, it was just as she told Edie Towler and me. She was going to go home and get the first real sleep she had enjoyed in years.

Sleep.

And so, literary Nina:

'Sleep, sweet sleep, that knits up the raveled sleeve of care.'

And why, Nina, didn't you see it? Edie? Edie is a businesswoman. A civic leader. She was thinking of the town.

But Nina, you should have been thinking about Hope.

Why didn't you realize what she was going to do?

Of course if you had, what would you have done? You could have told Moon Rivard, 'Moon, I think Hope Reddington is going to commit suicide.' And he would have asked...

...well he would have asked just what Helen was about to ask.

Right now.

"Nina..."

"Yes, Helen?"

"Nina, I got to grandmamma's house about nine-forty five. She was stretched out on the couch, the bottles of pills beside her. I called 911 and they got there fast. The orderlies said she was still alive and they gave her a shot of something, I'm not sure what it was. I followed them here and helped get her checked in. But Nina..."

"Yes Helen—I'm here, ask me whatever you need to."

"One of the nurses at the desk, a Ms. O'Leary?"

"Bridget. What about her?"

"She said that Grandmamma had been here. At the hospital, earlier in the evening, and that she had been talking to you and Ms. Towler. Nina, is that true?"

And there it was.

Of course the correct answer would have been:

'Yes, Helen, it is true. Your grandmother was here, and she talked to Edie and me for quite some time. What she was doing was, she was confessing. You see, it seems that your grandfather, Marshall Reddington, stole fifty thousand dollars from The Bay St. Lucy Hospital—by the way he did this because he needed to pay off gamblers in New Orleans—and he let Harrison Morgan take the blame for it. Harrison Morgan, you may remember, committed suicide but your grandparents were so scared of the gamblers that they still remained silent. They got what was coming to them though because your grandfather died an agonizing death from cancer and your parents were killed in an auto accident. This was simply the gods' way of making everything all right. If you're Greek, that is. And by the way, Cory Morgan, Harrison's son, is now here in Bay St. Lucy—his mother just died and so he's released from an oath he probably swore to her not to seek vengeance on the hospital and the town—anyway he's now here in Bay St. Lucy seeking vengeance on the hospital and the town. He's going to keep killing people—he just killed one a few minutes ago, actually—until I find out who really took the fifty thousand dollars and tell the press, so his father's name will be cleared. And since I now know—so does Edie, actually—who really did steal the money, I can go ahead and tell Chip Herndon the truth, which may make Cory Morgan stop killing people, but he'll have—even though he's in jail—a multi-million dollar wrongful death lawsuit against Bay St. Lucy Hospital and your grandmother. Unless she's dead. In which case he can sue you.'

And that would have been the truth.

"Helen—yes, she was here."

"But what did she say, Nina? Why did she come up here? I just saw her this morning and she seemed fine. Did something happen during the day? Surely if the two of you talked to her so recently, she must have given some indication that something was wrong, that something was depressing her, terribly. She's always been a good friend of yours, Nina. Whatever was driving her to do this terrible thing—she must have given some indication of it to you and Edie. Nina, what did my grandmother say to the two of you?"

Nothing of any consequence, Helen. She talked about the weather. The sleet. Of course she and I always talk about the weather and always have, even back to the time Frank and I were having dinner at your grandparents' house. Oooooh, loved those dinners. Yum. Yeah, she talked about that and she asked me how I was doing. And I'm doing pretty well, actually. Ankle isn't really very swollen. That warfarin is good stuff. Anti-coagulant you know. So no, there was nothing wrong that we could tell. She just sat here and chatted with us and then drove home and went into her living room and tried to kill herself. That's about it.

And that would have been a lie.

And Helen never would have believed it.

So what do you do, Nina?

You have to say something.

And so you say...

"Helen, yes she was here. And she wanted to talk about..."

"I'm sorry, ladies, but one of you is going to have to come with me!"

This from a uniformed policeman who had just appeared in the doorway.

He resembled a younger Captain Hall, and could even have been taken for Captain Hall, if Captain Hall had not just been shot dead in full view of the state of Mississippi and actually the rest of the country and, when one came to think about it, the rest of the whole world.

So he was not Captain Hall.

But he was exactly as tall as Captain Hall, and he had on the same Woodsman of the World uniform that Captain Hall had been wearing, and he even had started developing the same wrinkles and the same angles that had mapped themselves over Captain Hall's body.

Finally, he spoke with the same authority that had emanated from Captain Hall.

And so he repeated, this time clearly speaking to Helen:

"Ma'am, you're going to have to come with me down to the lobby."

Helen stared at him for a moment, incredulous.

Then, obviously doing all she could to fight back both tears and a growing sense of frustration and rage, she stammered:

"I'm Helen Giusti! My grandmother is in the next ICU room over—and she's fighting for her life!"

"I'm sorry, Ms. Giusti. But you'll have to come now."

"Who are you?"

"Lieutenant Travis, ma'am. Mississippi State Police."

"And just why do I have to go down to the lobby, when a woman I love is possibly dying in the next room?"

The lieutenant merely shook his head and said, in a voice that could have been filtered through a radiophone:

"The hospital is on lockdown mode."

"It's what?"

"Lockdown mode."

"And what does that mean?"

"It means only essential hospital personnel can be in these rooms and corridors. Everyone else, including all relatives and visitors, goes to the lobby, undergoes a security check, and is escorted out of the building."

"But that's my grandmother in there! Don't I have a right to…"

"We have a shooter in the building, ma'am."

"What?"

Nina interposed:

"Helen, while you were following Hope up here, an officer in the state police was shot. Apparently he was killed."

Confusion and frustration mounting, Helen was able to ask, "Who shot him? Was it this Cory somebody they've been talking about on the news?"

"It might be, Helen."

"Then—then we can't leave Grandmamma here!"

"You have to, Helen. She's in ICU. They're fighting to save her life. If she's moved, she'll almost certainly die."

"All right, I understand, but just tell me—my god, this is turning into a nightmare—at least tell me what Grandmamma said when she was talking to you and…"

But she was interrupted by the lieutenant, who stepped toward her and held out his hand, as though he were prepared to grasp her and pull her along with him should she refuse to go:

"Ma'am, we have to go to the lobby *now*! I'm sure the doctors and nurses are doing everything possible for your grandmother. And as for the shooter, officers are currently being stationed at short intervals along all the corridors. We're searching every room. We will find this man. But you'll make our job much easier by accompanying me now."

"All right, but could I not speak with one of the nurses…"

"No, ma'am, we have to go."

Nina attempted to be as reassuring as possible to Helen, who had risen and was making her way, as though she were a sheep being driven, to the door of the room.

"It will be all right, Helen."

"I don't know. I just…"

The lieutenant placed his hand gently on her upper arm:

"We need to go, ma'am.'

And then the doorway was empty.

Helen had been led away down the main corridor.

Which was filling up with armed policemen, some knocking on doors, others simply entering, guns drawn, what appeared to be empty rooms.

One policeman came into her room, though, and shook his head.

It was Moon.

"Hello, Ms. Nina. I thought I'd come and check on you."

"Moon! What in heaven's name is going on?"

"Lockdown. They checking everybody out but what they absolutely got to have."

"That man Travis though—he said there was a shooter in the building!"

"That's what they're thinking, all right."

"But that's impossible. Michael Yancy saw Cory Morgan escape from the building! He followed him out! There was a car chase at eighty miles an hour! We heard it, Moon!"

"I know we did."

"But why aren't they searching for him out there? If Michael Yancy.."

Moon merely shook his head and said:

"Michael Yancy, Ms. Nina, is under arrest."

CHAPTER NINETEEN: THE PHANTOM OF THE DUNES
11:00 P.M.

"He's what?"

"He's under arrest."

"For what?"

"I'm not too sure. But they're holding him downstairs."

"Who's holding him?"

"State police, Ms. Nina."

"But that's crazy!"

"I know, but there it is."

"What happened?"

"Well it...you mind if I sit down?"

"Of course, I don't mind. But shouldn't you be downstairs?"

"If I go downstairs, I might get arrested too."

"You're not making any sense. Moon, what happened?"

He sat, folded his hands on his stomach, and glanced at the television, which Nina had forgotten about. Chip Herndon was broadcasting again, eyes wider than ever.

"They reporting about Hall's death. Apparently the governor's talking about coming down in person. It's bigger than Columbine. Reporters are coming. And I don't just mean local guys like Herndon. No, ma'am. This is going national. When it was just the car exploding and the messages—that was one thing. But nobody else had actually got killed—at least not on national tv."

"Hall is really dead then?"

Moon nodded.

"Shot right through the heart. Police rifle."

"How did Cory Morgan get hold of a police rifle?"

"Pawn shop. Anywhere. This is Mississippi. All you have to have is a driver's license, and you can buy an AK-47 at any gun show."

"It's too bad about Hall though. I didn't like the man. And I didn't like what he was saying about you making all this stuff up."

"For a while he almost had me convinced."

"Well, he pretty quick got unconvinced."

"Yes."

"It's like I say though. It's not as though I liked the man. Never have. But nobody deserves to die like that. Shot like a deer or something. As it happens, from a second floor window of the hospital."

"They know that?"

"Found the shell casing."

"So Cory Morgan shot Captain Hall out of a hospital window, a window in a second floor room. And he was able to get into this room how?"

"Hole in time."

"What?"

"A hole in the time my men got ordered off the case and Hall's got deployed. For just those few minutes the hospital was pretty much unguarded."

"And Hall wasn't aware of this 'hole'?"

"Hall never believed there was a Cory Morgan here in the first place. And also, Ms. Nina, you had to know Hall. He was a very ambitious man. Me, I think he wanted to be governor someday."

"So this was just a big photo shoot for him."

"Yes, ma'am, and he wanted the state to see him out there, the great general addressing his troops."

"All right, I get all this. Cory Morgan shot Hall, took the rifle with him and left behind a shell casing. He took off down the stairway, out the back door and into a vehicle of some kind that he had left parked in back. Yancy, who had just been taken off the case like the rest of your men, was headed out of the hospital and back to your headquarters. He saw Cory leave, and he took off after him. The rest we heard."

"Yes, ma'am, we did. Except not all of it."

"So tell me the rest."

"Yancy lost Morgan in the dunes somewhere about four miles south of town."

"How could he just lose him like that?"

"Well, according to what he says, he was never really closer than half a mile. That's a pretty wild stretch of coastline out there and the dunes are like mountains. Night was dark as hell and the sleet won't seem to stop falling. That weather, those conditions—just no way to look for tire prints."

"All right. So he lost him. That still puts Cory Morgan four miles south of town and not back here in the hospital. Unless somebody thinks he turned around and came back."

Moon shook his head.

"No, ma'am, the state boys don't think he came back."

"Then what do they think?"

"They think he was never out there."

"What? But Michael…"

"They don't believe Michael."

Nina simply stared for a time, then said:

"But that's absurd! How could they not believe him?"

"Well, Ms. Nina, it's pretty easy to not believe him when you think about it."

"I'm thinking about it—and I still don't see why he's under arrest."

"You got to understand. They're state men and don't think much of my boys in the first place. Two of the officers making the chase were with Hall here in the room when he accused you of making it all up."

"Yes, I remember them."

"You also probably remember Hall insulting the kid and telling him to go home."

"Yes."

"So there's like four state squad cars that have been chasing after him out in the sleet storm, them not seeing nothing of any Cory Morgan, who Yancy says is driving eighty miles an hour with the lights off. When they get to him, he's standing out on a deserted stretch of huge sand dunes, telling them to start looking for this hidden car with a phantom red-haired shooter in it. Except they got no way to believe there was ever a car in the first place and they don't like Yancy giving them orders. Yancy—I got all this from Johnson you understand—kind of lost his cool. Started calling them names and such. They told him to come on back with them into town. Things escalated I guess, with him all the time insisting that Morgan had to be out there and them all the time insisting that he couldn't be and that Yancy was either drunk or crazy. Finally they just got sick of the thing and ordered him to drive back with them. He refused. And they arrested him."

"That's crazy."

"Yes, ma'am. But there it is."

"I don't—I just can't—"

She shook her head:

"Moon, do you believe Michael was just imagining all of this? He saw a man with flaming red hair running out of the hospital, he saw the man get into a car, and he followed him out to the dunes!"

"Well, that's what he said."

"And you don't believe him?"

"I believe the kid's under a lot of stress. We all are."

"But could he have made up this whole thing?"

"No, I don't think so. But there is one other way to explain it."

"All right, so tell me."

Moon pursed his lips and spoke quietly:

"Yancy was in the staircase. He saw somebody going out the back door, and, yeah, let's say that was really Cory Morgan. Yancy followed. He saw a vehicle of some kind pulling out onto Breakers Boulevard and he assumed Morgan was driving. He turned on his lights and started his siren."

"And the other driver just tried to get away."

"Happens all the time. We get high speed chases. But the car we're pursuing doesn't happen to be a killer, at least not always."

She breathed deeply and said, "Moon, I guess there's something I need to tell you about Michael Yancy."

There was something she needed to tell him—and the world—about Hope Reddington, too, but that could wait.

Maybe it could wait forever.

But for now, one secret at a time.

"Michael told me that, when he went into my shack to look for Furl…"

"Yes, Ms. Bannister?"

"He said he knew that Cory Morgan had been there before him. And he said he also knew that, before this night was over, the two of them would meet each other. And that he would kill Cory Morgan; or that Cory Morgan would kill him."

Moon sat for a time, apparently digesting this.

Finally he said, "If he thinks too hard about that kind of thing, then every hallway he walks down, every car he sees on the road…"

"…will have Cory Morgan in it."

"Yes, ma'am. Man's mind does funny things when it gets an idea stuck in it. Anyway, good that you told me that."

"Please don't tell Michael I told you."

"No, I won't. But I probably ought to go downstairs now and get the boy out of the state policemen's hands."

"You think they really arrested him?"

"No, not really. I think they felt like he was imagining things, and they needed to get him back here for his own good. Anyway, I'll do what I can to calm him down. Until then, there's ten state cops in every hallway. You'll be well guarded."

"Thank you, Moon."

And he left.

CHAPTER TWENTY: TELLING THE TRUTH (AND WHAT IT GETS YOU)
11:20 P.M.

The door was now closed, but through its small glass window Nina could see policemen coming and going. They were walking down the corridors, accompanied by nurses or orderlies, who were consulting various charts. This was, she assumed, to prevent a critically ill patient from having a door burst open and hearing, "I want to check your closet for a psychotic killer."

She allowed herself to be hypnotized by such activity, mixed with the scenes playing out on the television, which still sat flickering not far from her elbow.

Red lights, an ambulance, more emergency vehicles.

Where, she found herself wondering, was the body of Captain Hall?

Had it already been taken away?

Talking heads, interviews, politicians in black suits with red ties.

The sound was turned down. She did not need it, being able to imagine the words that were being said.

'We are doing everything possible to…'

'The Bay St. Lucy Hospital is now being guarded by the most highly trained security personnel.'

'Cory Morgan—if he is in fact the shooter, if he is in fact responsible for the earlier car bombing, will be found. And found quickly.'

But would he be found?

And how many people would be shot before that happened?

Also—could she put a stop to all of this merely by using her own telephone to contact Chip Herndon and clearing Harrison Morgan?

Would that really stop Cory's rampage?

Also, if…

But these musings were interrupted by the room door opening suddenly and Lalima Singh walking in, surgical mask hanging around her neck, clear plastic gloves still covering her forearms.

She walked briskly to the bed, put her palms down on the mattress, and said, matter-of-factly:

"I thought I should tell you firsthand about the condition of Ms. Reddington."

Nina held her breath for an instant, while through her mind flashed the thought, 'I don't want to know.'

But that thought dissolved quickly, as she knew it must, and she said quietly:

"Tell me."

Lalima Singh drew in a deep breath, hesitated only a moment, and said:

"I think she will recover."

Nina fought against the urge to cry.

Why cry now?

It's going to be all right!

Why cry?

So thinking, she cried.

Dr. Singh waited while she sobbed for a time, then took some tissues from her light blue smock and handed them to her.

"I'm sorry," said Nina, daubing her eyes.

"It's quite all right. Perfectly normal. You are under an intense emotional strain, as are we all. No. It was very close. If her granddaughter had not found her just in time, she would have been lost. Well, at any rate, we washed her stomach out by gastric lavage—stomach pumping—to mechanically remove unabsorbed drugs from the stomach. We then injected activated charcoal to help bind the drugs she had taken and keep them in the stomach and intestines. The drug, bound chemically to the charcoal, is then expelled in the stool. Once she regained consciousness—which she did some fifteen minutes ago—we were able to administer a cathartic so that she could more quickly evacuate the stool."

Nina was now close to the end of her sobbing.

Lalima Singh came closer though and spoke more softly, having become a human being instead of a medical textbook, "Something that I must ask you, though."

"Yes?"

"You know Ms. Reddington quite well, I assume."

"Yes, and for a long time."

"She has, since regaining consciousness, been speaking of you."

"What is she saying?"

It was at first largely incoherent. But as her mind cleared, so did her speech. 'Nina!' she keeps repeating. 'Nina has to tell them! I stole the money! Marshall and I stole the money, and now we're paying for it! Nina knows. Nina has to tell or God will keep punishing us! He'll keep punishing the whole community."

Silence for a time.

"Can't you," Nina asked, "give her a sedative? Let her sleep so she'll stop saying these things?"

"No! That is the last thing we want. We must make sure her ventilation system—that is her ability to breathe—functions well. That is the first duty of all physicians when it comes to drug overdoses. Also, she must continue to evacuate her bowels, which she will not do if sedated. So no, she must remain aware. But I also must ask you again: what is this money she is raving about? Can it have had anything to do with the reasons for her suicide attempt?"

"I don't…"

She was about to say, 'I don't know,' which would have been a lie, of course, but Lalima Singh interrupted her by standing up and saying:

"Nina, I think I must ask you a favor."

Thank heaven.

The lie postponed.

"What is it, Lalima? What do you want me to do?"

"Well, it is highly irregular, and normally I would never suggest it. Normally we forbid all visitors, even close relatives, to people in Ms. Reddington's stage of recovery. But she is so agitated at this time, that it may be possible for you to calm her."

"You want me to go over there and try to talk to her?"

"I do."

"All right."

"Good. I'll get a Latricia to come and push your bed over. We want to be sure and not disturb the IV. By the way, I assume your ankle is no longer bothering you."

"No, just murders, car explosions, high speed chases, and close friends trying to commit suicide. Oh, and invisible psychotic killers on the loose in the emergency ward. Other than that, I'm fine."

"Excellent," replied Dr. Singh, utterly oblivious to what Nina thought had been an approximation of humor. Of course, it was not humor; it was the bare truth.

But it is so strange, Nina found herself musing as Latricia and a younger nurse showed up to transport her, so strange how closely related those two things— humor and the bare truth—actually are.

Within minutes she found herself being wheeled into the adjacent ICU room and approaching Hope

Reddington, who was propped up in her own hospital bed, tubes streaming out of every body part.

"Nina!"

The woman's face was completely without color, but her eyes still sparkled, and she still seemed to be looking up and out from under something.

"Hope! Hope, how are you, dear Hope?"

What a stupid question, Nina.

Alive, that's how you are.

And just barely so.

"Nina, have you not told them yet? You and Edie— have the two of them not told them yet?"

"Hope," not-answered Nina, still trying to avoid the issue, "Hope you've got to try to get some rest. You took too many pills. Hope, we almost lost you!"

This merely elicited a shake of the head from Hope, who said, with even more urgency:

"It doesn't matter about me! This man is going to keep killing people. He's been sent from God, Nina, don't you see that?"

"There are police everywhere, Hope. They're going to catch him. They'll catch him any minute. These are the best security people in the state."

"It doesn't matter, Nina. He's like an angel sent down to make things right, because of our crime, the crime Marshall and I committed. The crime I told you and Edie about. Nina, is it true? You haven't told anybody, like I begged you to do? Why haven't you told someone?"

But before she could answer, 'No, we haven't," and before she could explain why they hadn't—namely that doing so would be disastrous in more ways than anybody could count—the door to the room burst open and Edie Towler burst in, followed by two state policemen, both of whom were saying essentially the same thing:

"Ma'am you can't…"

"… be in here now because the…"

"… hospital is on a lockdown mode and that means that no…"

"…body but essential personnel and patients are allowed to…"

Blah de blah de blah.

To which Edie merely replied, "I'm the President of the Hospital's Board of Directors. If you want, I can get the Governor of the State of Mississippi on the telephone—I can do that in about two minutes—and he can explain to you why I'm allowed entry into this hospital—and AT ANY TIME! Do you get that?"

A pause.

Neither state police officer seemed anxious to speak to the state governor.

"It's just that—ma'am, our orders are—"

"I'm giving you your orders right now! They are: leave! Leave right this minute and go catch Cory Morgan!"

"All right, ma'am, but…"

"LEAVE!"

And the two of them did so.

After which, Edie spoke to Hope, "Hope, I heard only a short time ago about what you tried to do. What were you thinking?"

"It doesn't matter about me, Edie."

"Of course it matters about you. You're the heart of Bay St. Lucy."

"I'm the curse of Bay St. Lucy."

"That's ridiculous."

"It's the truth. But Edie, I trusted you and Nina. Why didn't you tell the world what Marshall and I have done? Did I not make it clear to you?"

"Yes, you did, dear. You made it very clear."

"Well, then? Why didn't you do as I asked? Don't you realize what I've got to do now? Since you haven't told Mr. Herndon about all this, then I have to do so myself. An hour ago I can remember thinking, 'You've done it, Hope. You've told the vile secret to the most trustworthy of friends. They will pass it along. The sore will be opened, the poison will start draining out. Now all you have to do is go to sleep.'"

She merely shook her head and continued, "But it didn't work that way. You let me down, the two of you."

Edie was silent for a time.

So was Nina, who could only think:

Maybe it would have been better if the pills had worked.

Then the secret would have been safe.

Now...

But she was spared speculation about 'now' because Edie was taking care of it.

"All right, Hope."

Hope's head raised slightly off the pillow, and her eyes grew brighter:

"You'll do it? You'll tell everyone?"

Edie merely leaned down over the bed, saying, "No, Hope, you will."

WHAT? thought Nina.

Then she let the last few sentences that had been said repeat themselves in her mind and said to herself:

WHAT?

YOU WILL?

WHAT IN HEAVEN'S NAME COULD HAVE BEEN GOING ON IN EDIE'S HEAD?

But meanwhile, Edie was speaking softly to Dr. Singh, asking, "We need the reporter, Chip Herndon, to come and listen to Hope. Do I have your permission to bring him up here? And also her daughter, Helen."

"It is, you feel, absolutely essential?"

"Yes. It's our only chance to calm Ms. Reddington down. As it is, she's desperate."

"All right. Nurse O'Leary?"

Bridget O'Leary stepped forward, "Dr. Singh?"

"You recognize this Mr. Herndon?"

"I ought to. He's been on television all night."

"Then please go downstairs and see if you can locate him."

"Tell him," said Edie, "that he's got the biggest story of the night waiting for him up here."

"All right."

And, so saying, Bridget O'Leary left the room.

Nina pulled Edie into a corner while Hope allowed Dr. Singh to check her blood pressure, her catheter, her IV …

…etc., etc.

"Edie, what are you doing?" she whispered.

To which Edie merely shook her head, answering softly:

"It will be all right, Nina."

"*What* will be all right?"

"You don't need to worry."

Nina spoke louder, "Edie, are you listening to yourself? *You're* the one who's worried about million dollar wrongful death suits. *You're* the one who's worried about the hospital, the town. Look at what Hope's getting ready to do. She's going to admit to this wide eyed story-hungry reporter that she and her husband—both pillars of our community—railroaded an innocent man, a good man, and drove him to suicide. And the entire town stood by and watched this happen. Edie this will be front page news. And if you think the whole thing will devastate Bay St. Lucy, imagine what it's going to do to the Giustis, especially Helen, who has always idolized Hope. Are you thinking at all about these things?"

"Yes, Nina, I'm thinking about them. I have been thinking about them ever since Hope came into your room—what seems like days or months ago—and dropped this bombshell on us."

"And yet you're bringing Herndon up here so Hope can tell him the whole thing?"

"Yes."

"But, Edie, what are you thinking?"

"It will be all right, I promise you."

"*How* will it be all right? How will it possibly…"

She could not finish the sentence.

For at that moment, Bridget O'Leary entered the room, followed in turn by Helen Reddington—who threw herself into the tube- and needle-punctured arms of her grandmother—and Chip Herndon.

"Grandmamma!"

"It's all right, dear. It's all right, my dearest Helen."

"What were you doing? What were you thinking?"

"It would have been for the best, Helen. For you, for John—and for me. It would have been for the best."

"But that's absurd. John and I love you so dearly. Everyone in Bay St. Lucy loves you. Grandmamma, are you ill? Do you have some fatal sickness you haven't told us of?"

Hope shook her head and showed something like a wan smile.

"Not in the sense that you are imagining."

"Do you have cancer?"

"Again Helen, there are all kinds of cancers. There is one in Bay St. Lucy. It's eating away at the town, and no one knows it. Not yet anyway. But that will have to change."

"What are you talking about?"

At this moment, Chip Herndon stepped forward and said, "Ms. Reddington, I'm Chip Herndon."

"I know that, dear. I've watched you on television. What you're having to report is genuinely horrible."

"That's true, ma'am."

"But you do it in a professional manner."

"Thank you. I appreciate that. The nurse here, Ms. O'Leary, found me downstairs. She says you have a story that is extremely urgent, and that relates to the crimes that have been committed tonight here in the hospital."

"That's true."

"I am, of course, especially interested in any such stories. Are you sure though that you want to talk to me now? I'm aware that you've been through quite an ordeal…"

"It must be now. It must be right now."

"All right. Dr. Singh if you feel it's okay…"

"It may," said Lalima Singh, "be our best alternative. We shall, of course, continue to monitor all of the patient's vital signs."

"Of course. Well, then. I'm going to sit here by the bed. I do most of my note taking on my smart phone. There. It's on and ready, when you are."

Helen Reddington disentangled herself from her grandmother and sat in a second chair, saying as she did so, "Grandmamma, are you sure you're up to this?"

"Yes, dear. It's only not doing this that I am not up to. Now, Mr. Herndon, your reports have made clear that the Bay St. Lucy Hospital has been terrorized by a young man named Cory Morgan."

Yes, ma'am, that's true."

"And that this young man's father was convicted several years ago—ten, I believe—of embezzling money from the hospital. Fifty thousand dollars, I believe."

"Yes, Ms. Reddington, those are the facts as we now understand them."

"Well, then, I now must tell you: my husband and I stole that money. We did so in order to pay my husband's gambling debts."

There was a shocked silence in the room, a silence broken only by the hum of various slate gray and ice blue machines, and the continual muffled wail of sirens.

"Grandmamma!" stammered Helen Giusti. "What are you saying?"

"I'm telling the truth."

Chip Herndon, looking down at the glowing keypad, asked quietly, "Your husband managed to embezzle fifty thousand dollars without it being detected?"

"Yes."

"And how was he able to do that?"

"He was aided by Homer Baron Robinson."

"The gangster?"

"Yes. The gangster."

"And you've kept this silent for the last ten years?"

"You're coming forward now because…"

"Because I want Cory Morgan stopped. I don't want him killing any more people because of a crime my husband and I actually committed. I think Cory Morgan is an angel sent by God."

"An angel?"

"Yes. Sent because of our sins, and the town's sins."

Herndon nodded, typed something, then asked, "You committed the embezzlement even though overwhelming evidence was brought against Harrison Morgan. I was not reporting here at the time, but I've been able to check into the matter tonight. The facts did seem irrefutable. There was not even talk of appeal."

"Homer Baron Robinson—and his people—were very clever."

"I'm sure they were, Ms. Reddington. I'm sure they were. And you never told anyone about this crime that you and your husband committed?"

"No. New Orleans gamblers threatened our lives."

"You didn't report the threats to the police?"

"We were too scared."

"And which gamblers were these," he asked skeptically, "the ones who threatened you?"

"I don't know their names. We never knew their names."

"I see." His fingers tapped a little more. "Well, are there more facts you want to tell me?"

"No. That is the story. When will it be on television?"

Herndon turned off his smart phone and stood up, slipping his phone into his pants pocket.

"I'll have to call my editor. There are so many stories breaking now."

"I understand."

"But I'll certainly do what I can. A story this big— there are a number of facts to be verified."

"I understand that, too."

"But thank you so much for telling me all this. I can only imagine how difficult it must have been for you. I'm going now. And please, Ms. Reddington—do try and rest."

"Of course."

He left the room, motioning, as he did so, that Nina, Edie, and Helen, were to follow him into Nina's room.

Once there, Helen said, "Are you going to report this on television?"

But it was Edie, not Herndon, who answered, saying, "He's not going to put it on television at all, are you Mister Herndon?"

Chip Herndon shook his head.

Helen persisted.

"Why not?"

"Because it's the most absurd pack of nonsense I ever heard in my life." Herndon briefly smiled and left the room.

CHAPTER TWENTY ONE: BAREFACED LYING
(AND WHAT IT GETS YOU)
11:40 P.M.

Five minutes later, Edie and Helen were seated
around Nina's bed, in Nina's room, where Nina's brain
was still trying to make sense of things.

First there was Helen to be dealt with.

"Grandmamma now seems to be a little better, a
little more at ease."

"She had to tell her story," explained Edie. "She had
to get it off her chest. And she did."

"But Edie, Nina—surely none of that could be true."

To which Edie merely shook her head. "No. It's all
in Hope's head."

"Then, the time she spent with you, earlier this
evening—she was telling you this story?"

"Yes."

"And you simply let her go home? You didn't tell
anyone?"

Edie shrugged.

"There didn't seem to be anyone to tell."

"You could have called me."

"Yes, looking back, I assume that would have been
the proper thing to do. But at the time—Helen, the
hospital had become what it is now: a war zone. Your
grandmother was giving the two of us a kind of
ultimatum: we were to promise to tell Chip Herndon
everything, or she would do it herself. Finally, we
agreed to tell him. We never meant to do so. In short,
we lied to Hope. But once we told her that we would

reveal everything, she seemed to calm down. We got her promise that she would go straight home—she had come in a taxi—and that she would get some sleep. We didn't realize what she meant by 'sleep,' of course. She seemed distraught but certainly not suicidal. We also thought—and still do—that Cory Morgan would, by morning, be under arrest. We envisioned driving to your grandmamma's house early tomorrow morning, even waking her if we had to, and reassuring her, telling her that there would be no more murders. Upon hearing this, and seeing her yard, perhaps even a little blue sky, since the sleet storm is predicted to have ended—perhaps it would all have seemed like a bad dream, and she would even be able to laugh at herself and this fantasy that had been making her suffer."

Helen, seemingly somewhat pacified, nodded.

"I see that. But I don't see what could have driven her to make up a story like this. Is she—I don't even want to use the word—is she…"

Demented, thought Nina.

Exhibiting the signs of early Alzheimer's disease.

Crazy.

In exactly the same condition, that is, that Captain Hall had imagined her, Nina, to be in.

Helen kept trying, and failing, to produce the words.

"Is she…"

Edie nodded, reassuringly.

"I don't think so, Helen."

"She's been perfectly normal lately. She was out at the house only a few days ago. We cooked together, even did a crossword puzzle. And now she has these horrible delusions of something she and grandfather did a decade ago. As though he would have *ever* done such a thing. Or she, for that matter."

"Listen, Helen: I'm not a psychologist. But I think I know what Dr. Singh will suggest now."

"What?"

"You go home. I think you will be safe going downstairs and getting to your car, because there are police officers everywhere."

"I'm not worried about that. But grandmamma…"

"Is in the best of hands. They're monitoring her as closely as anyone can be monitored. After a half an hour or so, once all of her vital signs are stabilized, I feel certain they'll be able to give her something to help her sleep. She's told her story now and she feels relieved. We'll all see her early in the morning. But, with this young man in custody—which I'm certain he will be by then—the world will seem different."

"But if she still insists on these horrible things…"

"Then we'll all work together to find a doctor, and a treatment for her. But for now I think you should go in there, hug your grandmother, say good night to her, and persuade her to try to get some sleep as soon as the doctor thinks it's safe."

"Well, if you're certain that…"

A smile and a nod from Edie.

"I'm sure, Helen. Now you drive carefully, and we'll see you bright and early back here. The sun will be sparkling on the ocean, and this will all seem like a dream."

"All right. Good night then, both of you. And thank you for everything."

So saying, she left the room.

In the middle of which stood a huge pink elephant.

Nina ignored it for half a second or so.

But it did not go away.

And it would never go away.

It had to be dealt with.

Talked about.

So she talked about it, saying, 'Edie, there's a huge pink elephant in the middle of my hospital room, and..."

"... Edie, you're making everybody think Hope is crazy."

But Edie merely shook her head, saying, "I'm not making everybody think she's crazy; she is."

"But with our help."

"No! I do not accept that! You're not announcing to the world that Cory Morgan is an 'angel of vengeance sent down by God,' and neither am I. Listen, Nina: there's nothing either of us can do about this now."

"We can tell Chip Herndon we believe Hope."

"And *do* you believe her?"

"Edie, I talk with Hope almost every day, and have for most of my life. She's as rational as you or I."

"That's not the question I asked you. I asked if you believe her."

"I just...I don't..."

Edie leaned forward, and somehow added urgency to her voice:

"Nina, look out into the halls. Check the T.V. screen and look at what's going on outside. There is a small army here, looking into every storage closet and behind every tree trunk, all trying to find Cory Morgan. And I'll promise you, they *will* find him. They'll find him soon. And Nina bear in mind: this young man has just shot a captain in the state police with a long distance rifle as though the man were nothing more than a deer in rutting season. Do you know what these people are going to do with him when they find him? Do you?"

"I...I just don't..."

"You think they're going to 'interrogate' him and ask about his father, how his father was 'unjustly accused' and how he might be able to file an effective law suit? No, Nina, no, they're going to kill him. He's going to be dead within an hour."

"All right. But that doesn't mean we have to treat Hope like she's…"

"Demented? She made that diagnosis herself when she took those pills."

"She was desperate. Guilt ridden."

"Fine, so she was guilt ridden. But when she tried to commit suicide she destroyed any credibility she might have had."

"Edie, the woman wasn't lying and she wasn't demented. When she sat here not two hours ago and told her story, you yourself believed it, didn't you?"

"I just don't think I…"

"DIDN'T YOU?" Nina almost shouted.

"*All right*, I believed it. But it doesn't matter what I believed."

"How can you say that? This is *Hope* we're talking about."

"Fine, then let's talk about Hope. Let's talk about the whole situation. It's tomorrow at eight o'clock and the sleet storm has stopped. Cory Morgan is dead. His father is dead. His mother is dead. The hospital is secure, the town is secure. What good does Hope do by telling this story?"

"She gets peace of mind by finally telling the truth."

"All right then, she *has* told the truth. And no one believed her. So what are you and I going to advise her to do tomorrow morning, keep telling it? Ruining the last good years she's got left and what's already been a tragedy-filled life? Forcing her friends and loved ones to treat her like she's insane? Nina, if she continues to tell this story, they're going to lock her up. And her daughter, her beautiful and happy daughter, is going to spend the next years of her life visiting her 'grandmamma' in some kind of an asylum where she's on twenty-four hour suicide watch."

Edie paused then shook her head and said softly, "Nina, tomorrow you and I have got to convince her that tonight has been a bad dream. She's got to laugh about it and say she's made the whole thing up."

"But what if it's the truth?"

"It won't be. It will be the raving of an old woman. An old woman who can choose either to be a respected citizen of this town. Or the source of misery to all of her loved ones who can only shake their heads and wonder what happened to her mind."

Nina thought for a time.

Finally she was forced to nod.

"All right. I see the sense in what you're saying. There's no real reason for her to keep telling this story."

"All right. I'm glad you agree. Now I'm going home. I'm going to try to do what I just advised Hope and Helen to do—get some sleep. If you want, we can ask Dr. Singh to release you and you can come with me. I don't think you want to be here when they find Cory Morgan."

But Nina merely shook her head, saying, "No, I'm staying. Captain Hall may have been wrong about me making all this up; but he was right about one thing: Cory Morgan seems intent upon communicating through me. Somehow he still seems to trust me. Maybe by staying here I can help keep him alive—and maybe even keep him from killing anybody else."

"If you think that's what you want to do…"

"Actually, Edie, what I want to do is go crabbing. I want it to be summer, and I want to be out on the jetty."

"That sounds wonderful. We'll go together. But for now, I'll see you tomorrow morning. One way or another this will all be over. And Nina, one last thing:

what Hope told us is just a story, and doesn't have to go any farther."

"Yes, I agree."

"Good."

"And, so saying, Edie Towler left the room.

"It doesn't have to go any farther," Nina whispered to herself while mentally approaching the jetty.

The stone jetty which she loved.

"It doesn't have to go any farther."

Buttressed on each side by huge red slabs of rock, upon which and through which the great ocean waves roared and sifted.

"It doesn't have to go—it doesn't have to—"

All of the nurses and orderlies and police officers in the corridor were disappearing now, because she was far away from them. She was holding, quite gingerly, a string in her hands. At the other end of the string, submerged beneath eddying water and creviced between the cracks of rocks, illuminated green by a torch shining from the jetty, was a chicken breast impaled upon a wire.

"No further. The story—no further—"

There! There, just watch, Nina! Crabs, hidden in the rock fissures, are making their way to the meat and fastening onto it, claw-forcing it into the monster-like thing that was a mouth, oblivious to the fact that they were being pulled ever so carefully out of the ocean.

Drop them into the bucket; drop them into the bucket...

...and sleep Nina.

Maybe Michael Yancy was right after all.

Maybe Cory Morgan was far away, down the coast line, hiding in the dunes.

Sleep.

Go dream-crabbing.

Hope's tale is just that—a tale.

You don't have to worry about it anymore tonight.

No more visitors tonight.

No need to believe the story or think any more about tonight.

Just go to…

But even as she said these words, her phone was beginning to buzz.

She popped it open and said:

"Nina."

The deep voice on the other end said:

"Nina this is Jackson Bennet. I have to talk to you. Immediately if not sooner."

"Why, Jackson?"

A pause. hen:

"I've just heard Hope Reddington confess to stealing fifty thousand dollars."

CHAPTER TWENTY-TWO: THE IMPORTANCE
OF CLEAR AND EFFECTIVE COMMUNICATION
11:50 P.M.

Within fifteen minutes, Jackson Bennet was sitting beside her bed, a small tape recorder engulfed in his massive hand.

"I'm sorry to bother you like this, Nina. Were you asleep?"

She fought the urge to laugh.

"No. I was on the stone jetty, fishing for crabs."

"Pardon?"

"Don't worry about it—bad joke."

"Well, anyway, you know I wouldn't bother you if it wasn't urgent."

"I know that, Jackson. So what is it?"

"I got a phone call half an hour ago."

"From?"

"Cory Morgan."

A pause to let this sink in.

Finally, Nina said, "That's not possible."

"Yes, it is."

"But Jackson, just look. Look out in the corridor. Look around the grounds of the hospital. There are a thousand policemen."

"I know. Most of whom I had to pass through to get up here. And I wouldn't have gotten in at all if I hadn't convinced a couple of first lieutenants that I was representing the hospital and had crucial papers for the doctor in charge to sign."

"Are there any such papers?"

He shook his head.

"Not now, Nina. But there will be, I can promise you that."

"Why? What papers?"

"There will have to be…well, first things first."

"Yes. And first is this call you said you got."

"I didn't just say I got it; I got it."

"From a young man who's being hunted by the entire state police force?"

"That's right."

"Jackson, where in God's name was he calling from?"

Another shake of the head.

"I asked him that and he refused to answer. Said it was of no importance. But he was calm as you please. For all I could tell, he was calling from the Sands Hotel in Las Vegas."

"This doesn't make sense. Unless he *is* a ghost. What did he say, Jackson?"

"He asked to speak to Jackson Bennet the attorney. I told him that was me. He said, 'This is Cory Morgan calling. I was stunned, as you might believe. I tried to tell myself it was a joke. But there was something about the voice—anyway I had no choice but to believe the caller was who he said he was. Then with that same terrifying calmness he said: 'I've just shot dead a Mississippi State Police officer.' I told him he needed to turn himself in immediately because there was a massive man hunt on for him all through Bay St. Lucy. I also told him these officers had just seen their captain shot and that they were not about to ask questions. If he showed himself, they would certainly kill him. But none of that seemed to bother him. He began to talk about his mother."

"Who just died of cancer," Nina added.

"Yes, a few days ago, or so he said. He also said he had made a promise to her not to come to Bay St. Lucy, even though that town had killed his father. But she was dead now. And he was here."

"But where, Jackson? He seems to be everywhere and nowhere."

"I don't know. But the person I was talking to on the phone certainly didn't seem to be a ghost. Anyway, I found myself pleading with him. 'Turn yourself in to me!' I told him. I also told him I could guarantee his safety during the arrest process. But he didn't even seem to hear me. He just said: 'I know who stole the money.' I couldn't believe that. If we couldn't find out the truth of that crime ten years ago, I didn't see how he could know it now. And I told him just those words. But he just cut me off in the middle and said, again calm as you please: 'I have it all on tape.'"

Jackson Bennet leaned forward then, and held out the small recorder.

"And he did have it all on tape. Once he began playing it, I had no choice but to keep listening. Finally, I asked him to replay it so I could make my own recording. Here. Listen."

He pressed a button.

There was a hissing sound, a bit of static.

And Hope making her confession.

Word for word.

Interrupted from time to time, first by Nina, then by Edie.

All of it.

Clear as a bell.

"We had been in Bay St. Lucy for some years. Our daughter was eight. The pharmacy was doing well, and Marshall had been for almost two years on the hospital's board of directors. But he had also come under the influence of Homer Baron Robinson."

"What could Marshall have had in common with that man?"

"Gambling."

"I always thought Marshall had no vices."

"There are no men with no vices—and probably no women either.

"We are all as God made us. And some of us, much worse."

"Not very much worse, not my Marshall. But a little. A little. And as for vices, well, I suppose we would have to add one more to his list."

"That one being?"

"Ambition. He wanted to 'be' somebody in Bay St. Lucy—"

And on and on.

The nightly card games at the Robinson Mansion... long weekends in New Orleans.

And—

Marshall, whether at the track or in expensive rooms in The Monteleone Hotel, was gambling with ever larger sums of money.

And—

The hospital was short fifty thousand dollars."—

And—

"There was also a human finger."

—until the recording finally ended, mercifully, with the words:

"And now Cory has returned. The crime goes on and on. The cycle does not end."

Finally, Nina could only ask:

"So now what are you going to do with this tape, Jackson? Are you going to ruin the Reddingtons?"

He shook his head:

"I'm not going to do anything to hurt Hope or Helen."

"But if you reveal this…"

Jackson merely held up one hand, palm out toward Nina. He then slipped out of the chair, got down onto the floor, and crawled forward until the upper part of his body was under the bed. She could hear the springs rattling.

When he stood up, he was holding a silver metal disc.

"Transmitter," he mumbled.

Nina could only shake her head and say:

"Everything that's been said in this room…"

Jackson nodded:

"…he's heard."

"But how did he plant that thing under there?"

"There's only one possibility that I can see, Nina. He has to have disguised himself as an orderly. Orderlies come and go. Maybe you went to the bathroom."

The bathroom?

Yes, maybe.

Or…

Come on, Jane…

A mind lively and at ease…

…don't be at ease.

"There is another possibility," she said.

"All right—tell me."

"Maybe he had help."

"What kind of help?"

"Maybe one of the nurses."

"Why would she help him?"

"Maybe she has no choice. Jackson, this man had Edie Towler believing that he had murdered her father. Maybe he's threatening to kill somebody else, somebody he's kidnapped. A husband maybe…"

"—and the wife, a nurse in the hospital, has got to do what he asks."

"That would also explain the switched IV bag," she continued, "and it would explain how he knew about the 'hole in time,' when Moon's men were relieved and Hall's were out there uselessly in formation, leaving the hospital unprotected."

"That would make sense, Nina. But there are two problems I've got to talk about with you now."

"All right."

"The first is, how anybody is going to identify this spy/nurse. She almost certainly can't identify herself— even if interrogated—or her loved one—husband, child, whoever—will die."

"Okay, I see that problem. And, no, I can't solve it. At least not right now. But what's the other one?"

He scraped his chair a bit closer to her and spoke more softly, as if he feared the presence of yet more microphones in the room:

"Nina, this woman made her confession to you and Edie Towler?"

"Yes. About two hours ago."

"And you did nothing about it?"

"What were we supposed to do, Jackson?"

"You were supposed to *tell* someone!"

"We tried to. Or rather, we tried to let Hope tell Chip Herndon. After she was brought into the ER, she kept raving about the crime and the money. So, when we knew she was out of danger, we had Herndon brought up here to Hope's bedside. She made the entire confession to him."

"And?"

"He didn't believe it, Jackson. He thought she had made the whole thing up. And you have to admit, it is pretty hard to believe."

"All right, so Herndon didn't believe her. What was your next plan?"

"What do you mean?"

"Who do you tell next?"

"No one."

"You tell no one! Hope Reddington admits that her husband, with the aid of Homer Baron Robinson, has embezzled fifty thousand dollars and blamed an innocent man—a man, by the way, whom your husband defended—and the two of you are just going to ignore her confession? Nina, look at yourself. You're one of the leading citizens of Bay St. Lucy. Everyone looks up to you. And if there's a second leading citizen, it's Edie Towler."

"I know, but…"

"But what? How can there be a 'but'?"

"There can be a 'but' because of what you yourself had told us only an hour or so before about the law. If all of these things come out—well, they can be devastating for the hospital, and for all of Bay St. Lucy. You yourself told us, Jackson, that Cory Morgan would be in the position to bring a million dollar wrongful death lawsuit against not only Hope but against the entire city. I lie here and I think about the headlines: 'Bay St. Lucy shooter driven to murder! (Because father driven to suicide!) Jackson, the town would be devastated—and Helen and John would never get over it!"

He nodded and said:

"All right, I see all of that. But, Nina, when you called me earlier in the evening and asked about convicted criminals being able to bring suit, I had no idea that you were talking about a real situation. If you'll remember, I told you that if you knew about someone else taking this money, that you would not be required to say anything. But I also asked you if the two of you knew anything about this matter. Neither of you said anything."

"Jackson, we just…"

"You had what you felt were valid reasons for keeping quiet. I understand that. You had what you felt to be the town's best interest, and the Reddingtons' best interest, at heart. I can understand that, too. But I hope you remember that I *would* be required to report anything I knew about the matter. I am an officer of the court. If anyone comes into my office and says, 'I've committed a crime,' then I must persuade that person to surrender to the police. If the person refuses, then it's my duty to report the crime. And, of course, I'm going to do it. I have to do it."

"Even if it destroys Hope, Helen, and John?"

"It won't destroy them."

"How can you say that?"

"I can say it because it's true. Nina, it's not publicizing this confession that's going to destroy the Reddingtons; it's keeping the confession quiet that's going to do that. And not only the Reddingtons, but Bay St. Lucy itself. This monstrous crime has existed here, festered here for ten years. Lives have been ruined because of it. Lives are continuing to be lost because of it. And all because of one criminal."

"And so you're going to a judge tomorrow and tell him that all of this suffering has been caused by Marshall Reddington."

But he merely shook his head in frustration and said:

"You still don't understand."

"I don't understand what?"

"The suffering wasn't caused by Marshall Reddington. He's not the criminal here. And if there is a million dollar wrongful death lawsuit to be brought, it should not be brought against Marshall Reddington."

"Then who…"

"It should be brought, Nina, against Homer Baron Robinson."

CHAPTER TWENTY THREE: IF THAT THOU
BE'ST A DEVIL, I CANNOT KILL THEE
11:55 P.M.

"Jackson," said Nina, "I don't understand. Hope's
confession is clear. Marshall loved gambling. Through
Homer Baron Robinson he met some powerful—and
dangerous—gamblers. He lost heavily to them—
$50,000 dollars. They were threatening his life.
Robinson arranged to have the books of the hospital
altered so that it would look like Harrison Morgan stole
the money. But he really managed it so that Marshall
Reddington could get the money, pay the gamblers, and
get off the hook. For this he was deeply indebted to
Robinson, but he had to promise to keep his mouth
shut, and say nothing about the gamblers, who did not
want their identities revealed."

But upon hearing this, Jackson Bennet merely shook
his head:

"I'm almost certain, Nina, that's not the way it
worked."

"I don't understand."

"Neither did Marshall Reddington. And therein lies
the great tragedy, the great sadness."

"But..."

"Do you remember how Homer Robinson died?"
Jackson asked.

"Of course I do. The whole town does. He was
murdered."

"But not by gangsters."

"No, he was murdered by his eldest daughter, whose life he had made miserable."

"And there's the secret. Frank and I both looked into this matter closely. I had just come to work for him, and he asked me to find out all I could."

"All right, but I still don't see…"

"Nina, Homer Robinson was not murdered by gangsters because he was never connected with gangsters."

"Then who did Marshall Reddington…"

"Gamble with in New Orleans? Almost certainly he gambled with people on Robinson's payroll."

"Then he lost the money…"

"To Homer Baron Robinson. And when Robinson cooked the books, the money went directly to him and not to any gamblers."

She was beginning to see.

"So in effect…"

"Robinson stole the money. And in doing so, in carrying out his plan, he did three things."

She interrupted, saying:

"Let me see if I've got it. First, he destroyed Harrison Morgan."

"The new man in town, and a man who wouldn't go along and allow himself to be manipulated."

"Right. Second, he put Marshall Reddington in his debt for life by convincing the man he had interceded with these 'dangerous gamblers'."

"…who were really just Robinson's stooges all along."

"True. And third?"

"Third, he just made himself fifty thousand dollars richer, at the expense of Bay St. Lucy and its hospital."

"You've got it. Frank and I might have been able to see through this at the time, because we already knew a little about Robinson and his dealings. But Marshall

Reddington was too terrified to seek advice from anybody, and Harrison Morgan had no idea what had happened to the money."

"So Hope has felt guilty all of these years…"

"…for no reason. She was a victim just as her husband was."

"But Marshall Reddington really did lose the money…"

"In what was certainly a rigged poker game. He was played for a sucker."

"My God. This is all just so…"

She was interrupted by the buzzing of the phone.

She flipped it open and pressed it against her ear, then said:

"This is Nina."

And from the other end came the words:

"Hello, Nina, this is Cory. Look at the clock: it's almost midnight. I think it's time to end our little game."

CHAPTER TWENTY FOUR: MIDNIGHT
12:00 Midnight

"I see," said the voice that was now rasping into her ears, "that you've found my little listening device."

"Yes. How did you manage to get it into this room?"

She turned the phone volume up so that Jackson could hear the words:

"I had help."

"Who helped you? One of the nurses?"

"Oh no."

"Then who?"

"One of the policemen."

"But that's crazy! Which policeman?"

"Why young Yancy of course."

"Michael?"

"The very same. He's been my eyes and ears for the entire evening. And by the way, he likes and respects you very much. At each one of our meetings he has insisted, 'I'll only help you if you promise not to harm Nina Bannister. She's a real lady."

"But he—he chased you!"

"He did and that was such fun! But, of course, I never turned onto the dunes as he reported. I kept going, then turned around and headed back to Bay St. Lucy, which, of course, is where I find myself now. As I proceeded, at a moderate speed, back into town, I could see the flashing lights of police cars over by the beach, searching for me. As I say, it was all great fun."

"Why would Michael Yancy agree to help you?"

"Because I know things about him. One thing in particular that he does not wish made public."

"What thing?"

"Oh, but that would be telling, would it not? No, that little item must remain between Michael and myself for just a bit longer. First things first though, as they say. As unfortunate as it is that my little listening device is of no more use to me, it did its job. I heard Herndon refuse to run Hope Reddington's confession. I also heard Jackson Bennet—who had the entire confession on a tape which he made from my tape—also refuse."

"But Jackson didn't..."

"Oh yes he did, Ms. Bannister. He said, quite clearly, 'I'm not going to do anything to hurt Hope or Helen.' Those were the last words I heard before one of you, I'm not sure which one, found my device. But those words are enough. Bear in mind, I was also able to hear your conversations with Mayor Towler, in which she refused to let the truth of this matter come out. No, the truth would be too painful, so the town—even the town's most 'moral' leaders, Edie, Jackson, and yourself—refuse to admit the truth. And indeed, why do so? My father is dead; my mother is dead; and you all expect me to be dead before morning."

"You don't have to be dead before morning. Just give yourself up."

"Oh I plan to. Precisely ten minutes from now. At that time I shall pay you a visit, Nina. I shall walk down the main corridor leading to your room. And because I am invisible, no one will see me. Not until I am actually standing by your bed. Being invisible has so many advantages, you see. I've learned all about them, those little advantages. I've had ten years to do so. I've inherited my invisibility. From my father and mother, who became invisible the night before my father was to be sent—wrongfully—to prison."

She did not know anything appropriate to say to this, and could only stammer, "All right. So you're coming to my room at midnight. What do you want?"

"Just what I've always wanted. For you to tell Bay St Lucy the truth."

"But we're going to, Cory. There's no reason not to now."

"Unfortunately, I don't believe you. I think that, as soon as I materialize in your room, I'll be arrested. Or I'll be shot. Because I'm a murderer, you know. I shot Captain Hall. And I enjoyed doing so."

"Why did you shoot him?"

"Because he was going to tell lies about you, Nina. He was going to say that I existed only in your mind, and that you were making all of this up. He was going to say that you were insane, whereas the truth is, I'm the one who is insane. Oh yes, quite insane. Insanity is a side effect of invisibility. It makes killing fun. And so I killed Captain Hall. I also murdered the person whose body you found in the burned car."

Even though she hated to do so, she could not stop herself from asking:

"Whose body was that, Cory?"

"All in good time. I've heard, during these my last hours in Bay St. Lucy, that you're very good at solving riddles. Strange that you've not solved this one, 'the mystery of the burned up body,' or so we might call it. But enough of this. It's midnight. The time has come, the walrus said, to talk of many things. Cabbages and kings, cabbages and kings. Cabbages: my co-conspirator Officer Yancy will arrive in your room within the next minute. And you must not be too hard on him. As I said, he had no choice in what he did tonight. As I told you, I know a terrible secret about him. The worst secret imaginable. And kings? He will have with him the beautiful Helen Reddington, whom he met downstairs, just as she was getting ready to drive home. I'm sorry to say, he lied to Ms. Reddington. He told her that her grandmother's condition was worsening, and that the old lady insisted on seeing her—and even kissing her for one final time—before she gave up life."

"Cory, why do you want Helen here?"

"Because I want Mr. Jackson Bennet to call Mr. Herndon and swear that Hope Reddington's confession is one hundred percent true. And I want to watch Mr. Herndon appear on television and report the truth."

"But what does that have to do with Helen?"

"Only that if Mr. Jackson refuses, or if Mr. Herndon refuses, or if one of many policemen stationed around your door attempts to arrest me after I materialize—and I must say, my materializations are quite dramatic—if any of these things should happen, I will be forced to kill her."

CHAPTER TWENTY-FIVE: OF CABBAGES AND KINGS
12:15 A.M.

The phone went dead.

Nina looked at Jackson and said:

"How can he 'materialize'?

"I don't know. But I know that any stranger, especially a red-headed one, who sets foot in this hallway is going to be arrested, or shot on sight. I can't understand how…"

He was interrupted by the entrance of Michael Yancy, followed by a distraught Hope Reddington, who, on the verge of tears, was able to stammer out the question:

"My grandmamma! This officer stopped me downstairs and told me she had taken a turn for the worse!"

Nina shook her head and said, quietly:

"This officer lied to you."

Then, to Michael Yancy:

"Didn't you, Michael?"

He looked at Helen and nodded, saying, "Yes, ma'am. I'm afraid I did."

"But—but why would you lie to me about a thing like that?"

Nina answered, saying, "He had no choice. Did you, Michael?"

"No, Nina. I had no choice."

"I've just spoken to Cory Morgan."

"Yes. I know."

"Do you know what he told me?"

"He told you that he was going to come in this room about now. He was going to make sure that Mr. Bennet told Mr. Herndon the truth about who really stole the fifty thousand dollars. He was also going to make sure that Mr. Herndon broadcast the entire story on television. And that if all these things didn't happen, he was going to kill Ms. Reddington."

Helen gasped, "Kill me?"

"Yes. At least that's what he told me he was going to do."

At this point, Jackson Bennet stood up—all six foot three inches of him, walked to the door, and peered out into the corridor.

"I count eight state policemen out there, Ms. Reddington. There is no way that anyone's getting into this room. There are no such things as ghosts. So you're safe here, believe me."

"But what did the officer mean about the 'real truth,' concerning grandmamma? Surely it's like we said: all those things she said following her suicide attempt, all those things about her and grandfather stealing the money and letting Harrison Morgan take the blame..."

Nina interrupted, saying: "They're true, Helen. And at the same time, they're not true. They are, at the same time, a delusion that has entrapped the mind of your grandmother for all these years."

"I don't understand!"

Jackson, still standing at the doorway, his eyes fixed on the silent corridor, said over his shoulder, "Your grandparents were tricked, Ms. Reddington. They were tricked by a ruthless man named Homer Baron Robinson. He stole the money and used it to line his own pocket. Then he made both your grandfather and your grandmother think that the fifty thousand dollars was being used to pay off your grandfather's gambling debts. Debts which, in reality, never really existed."

Michael Yancy took the service revolver out of its holster and let it hang by his side.

"You're not," said Jackson, "going to need that. There's nobody in sight out there except policemen."

"That may be," answered Yancy. "But it's like I said earlier. I have this strange feeling that we're going to meet. I'm going to kill him—or he's going to kill me. And if that happens, it might as well be now, and it might as well be in this room."

"All right, suit yourself. But it's like I say—the hallway is empty of anyone except a lot of cops."

Helen looked then at Jackson and asked, "So Mr. Bennet—are you really going public with all of this?"

"I certainly am. I'm calling Herndon now and giving him my personal assurance of the story's truth. There's no way he doesn't broadcast it, probably in the next hour. Then tomorrow morning I'm going to do what I told Nina and Edie Towler earlier in the evening that I'm required to do as an officer of the court. I'm taking this tape to a federal judge. The money is gone. Harrison Morgan and his wife are dead, and so is Homer Baron Robinson. But the truth needs to come out."

Helen nodded, saying, "I understand. But Grandmamma…"

Nina answered her.

"She'll be immensely relieved, Helen. She's lived all these years beneath the crushing guilt connected with a crime she never committed. Now she'll be free. It's like in the old Greek myths. The furies are guilt. They're wild dogs that tear remorselessly at people who commit crimes. Those dogs will go away now, and she can live out her life in peace."

Jackson Bennet said softly, "So in the end, Cory Morgan will have gotten all he wanted. He will have cleared his father's name. I don't approve of what he's done. But if he does manage to show up here without getting himself killed, I would be happy to defend him. I can't keep him out of jail. But with the right psychologist, I think I can put forward an effective insanity plea."

Upon hearing this, Michael Yancy merely shook his head.

"I don't think Cory Morgan will be showing up here, Mr. Bennet. I do think he's insane—but he's not going to be pleading for anything. It's like you just said: he's accomplished what he came to Bay St. Lucy to do. Now he's just going to go away."

Nina said, "I don't see how he can get away, Michael. There's a statewide search out for him."

"He'll find a way. He's very close to getting away right now."

"I don't understand."

"You will, Nina. And by the way, it's been a privilege to know you. I'm sorry I had to deceive you and be Cory Morgan's eyes and ears."

"That's all right, Michael."

"It's just that he knew something terrible about me."

"Can you tell me what that something is, Michael?"

He smiled grimly.

"He knew that I was murdered yesterday and chained to the back seat of a car that exploded. He knew that I was dead."

And so saying, Cory Morgan put the barrel of the gun in his mouth and pulled the trigger.

EPILOGUE
One week later.

A dinner invitation at the Giustis' house which she always loved going to, on the beach, up the coast from Bay St. Lucy.

Driving there now with John Giusti in the Veterinarians' van.

Nina's ankle was not swollen now, and no blood clot likely, or so said Dr. Lalima Singh—a new friend now to have coffee with, along with Bridget O'Leary, Judy Denf and Latricia Smith.

So many good things to take away from her long night in the hospital.

But some horrible one's too. Images she would never forget and could not stand to think about.

And so she simply rode along, enjoying the ride of what must have been ten miles, along coastal and not-so coastal roads that she'd never explored.

During these miles she entered a kind of coma, the not-quite-conscious state that she could recall experiencing—not without a kind of pleasure—as a child, when taken on long automobile trips in the rain. There was kind of a sound the windshield wipers made—which, like the smell of tomato plants on your hands after you'd picked and prodded at the lush green plants, or the taste of morning when it was a perfect morning—there were all these sensations that both isolated you completely while making you one with something else in the universe that was perfectly rare, utterly impossible to duplicate, and unimaginably common.

And for a time she simply breathed softly on the window glass while the yellow-pine forest wrapped itself around her.

The engine, which had seemed to be exploding at first, was now merely growling. The moon rose, horrible-red and massive—and the highway, now roadway, now dirt path meandered inward and downward.

They'd left the coastline for a few miles, she realized, and were now heading back toward it.

There—something darted across in front of them.

A deer.

Had that been a deer?

It was getting darker. Craning her neck, she could see the stars up through the roof of pine needles. The Mississippi sky was ferocious and black, stars glittering in mute and yellow explosions.

It all remained like this for a period out of time, all changes elemental and thus of great and no importance, until they reached the house.

"So here we are!"

"John, I love this place!" she said.

"We kept telling ourselves we need to have you out."

"Well, now I'm out."

"Indeed you are."

She had said the house was great because that was obviously the thing to say in this circumstance. In truth, she could not quite see the house, at least not clearly. But it was certainly as she remembered it to be. The path from the driveway led up to it, not down, and there were thick shrubs and trees everywhere.

Where was the ocean?

She could hear it, rumbling and grating not more than a few yards over the top of the trees; but she could only see a small yard, and the huge Labrador, jumping on John as he wrestled open the gate.

"We're home!"

"Remind me, how did you find this?"

"I had a client who lived here. I drove out to take care of one of the animals that was too sick to move. Fell in love with the place. The client moved away a few months ago and asked me if I was interested in buying it. I brought Helen out, and she fell in love with it. Look, would you mind waiting here by the van just a minute or so? There are some animals inside the fence that I need to pen up."

"Definitely pen up the animals."

"It won't take long, and I'm sorry to make you wait…"

"Definitely pen up the animals."

"All right. I'll leave you and this big guy to get to know each other."

He helped Nina down from the van, then strode off toward his house.

She walked a few steps behind him, still quite unable to see the shape of the dwelling, so masked was it by vegetation.

She noticed a bench by the walkway; she sat down upon it and began communicating with the Labrador retriever.

"Hello, boy," she whispered, petting a head which resembled a bowling ball.

"I love you," replied the dog in its own language, resting the remainder of its head upon her knee and salivating on the hem of her blue jeans.

"Nina!" came a shout from the house, "You can come on now. Just stay on the concrete path, and don't mind the trees!"

She rose.

The dog worked his way between her legs, planting a paw the size of a bullfrog atop one of her shoes and driving it into the soft earth.

"That's all right; that's all right, boy."

She made her way back toward the door of the house, while the dog ran around and through her like a canine mountain stream.

"Come on through here! It's a little tricky when it's wet."

She made her way along a twisting narrow sidewalk, the limbs of pine trees reaching out to brush against her, and she felt as though she were walking through the Black Forest.

Finally, the trees gave way and she could see.

"Wow!" she could not help exclaiming.

For there, laid out before her, was the wide, long, pier, at the end of which glowed like what would have been a magnificent beach house, had it been on the beach.

It was not.

It was an ocean house, perched as high above the surging waves—twenty feet or so, she judged—as her own shack was perched above the beach.

John, Helen, and Hope stood in the doorway, beckoning.

The house, all vast glass windows, seemed to reflect a thousand images of the three, the animals around them, and the sea beneath them.

Nina started forward, feeling the pier wobble a bit under her, boards swaying ever so slightly as she walked upon it.

The moon, perfectly jovially white, laughed at her.

"Come on out, Nina! The pier won't fall!"

"John!" she shouted back, trying to make herself heard over the grating and roaring of the waves, which became deeper more sweeping as the water deepened. "John, this is magnificent!"

"It's a good place, isn't it?"

She turned. The beach was behind her now, narrow but perfectly white, dark pine forests impinging upon it, as though the trees were trying to drive the sand into the water.

"Come in! Come in!" shouted Hope and Helen in harmony.

She stepped inside.

And in so doing she stepped outside.

For there was, strictly speaking, no inside.

There was the furniture. Heavy, mahogany, leather, couches tables chairs rugs and things a man would have to sit on and lie on and put things on and have some woman come in from time to time and clean.

But she was still more outside than inside, the vast glass walls magnifying everything on the coast, from birds that skimmed low over the ocean to lights twinkling miles to the south in Isle au Pitre, to slowly moving freighters that made their way like moving oil splotches hurled upon the clean azure evening sky and now oozing horizontally along it—to the waves, always the waves, swelling, throbbing, falling, and rising again, having vowed never to allow stillness to anything in the universe.

There was a time of group hugging and mass greeting.

Finally, she extricated herself sufficiently to ask:

"How far out are we, again, John?"

He beamed.

"Maybe a hundred and fifty feet."

"This is incredible."

"I know. Like I say, we fell in love with it when we saw it."

They were standing in the kitchen now—for it was a kitchen, and a modern one, with soft white light coming from a fluorescent tube above the oven, and a vast glass wall to their left showing an epic film version of The Ocean by Moonlight.

"It was supposedly built," said Helen, "by an architect who drank himself to death."

"But not while he was designing it, I hope. We're not going to fall into the water, are we? The poles aren't going to give way?"

"Haven't yet!"

This place is wonderful!"

And it was. The walls were doors, the roofs were walls, and air seeped in from everywhere, delightfully cool, whispering out of hidden crevasses that served as ventilation ports. There were animals all around, of course, most of them dogs, but cats here or there, and slinking little reptiles that peered around crags in the wall structure or out from gurgling fissures.

"Come on out!"

John opened a massive sliding door and the four of them stepped out into what seemed like empty space.

She followed, expecting to fall to her death, sucked into the surge below.

This did not happen, though, and she soon realized that, if she were in fact to drown, it would be as a result of spray flying up from collisions with the support poles beneath.

John's beaming face glistened with moisture.

"You still like it?"

"It's amazing!"

"The Mississippi coast," he said proudly, "is one of the most diverse in the country, in terms of pure ecology. Forests everywhere. But hey, let's sit down. We set the table out here to celebrate the wonderful weather we've been having after that awful stretch with its rain and sleet. We've got shrimp for starters, too. And I've been waiting to ask you, Nina—what is in that mysterious brown bag you've been unsuccessfully trying to hide in your purse."

She smiled as she took it out and put it on the table, saying:

"It's an excellent bottle of red wine. Some of the hospital staff bought it for me when I checked in."

John opened the bottle and poured a glass for each of them while Nina, ever the literary Nina, quoted:

"The King sits in Dunferline toun,
  Drinkin' the blude-reid wine."

Helen smiled. "Oh, the poem. "Sir Patrick Spens." I remember when you taught it to us."

"We're not in Dunferline town though, are we?" asked Hope. "We're in Bay St. Lucy. And I see it in a way I haven't been able to for years."

"The stories," said Nina, "have all been very supportive of you and Marshall."

"They would have to be," added Helen. "You were both victims of a very bad man."

"Yes," said Hope, eyes sparkling, looking up and out over the crystal sea, "there have been so many cards of solace. I only wish Marshall could have been here to see his name cleared."

They were silent for a time.

Finally, Hope continued:

"I feel like such a great burden has been lifted. But at the same time, I feel a great sadness for the young policeman Yancy."

"Yes," said Nina, quietly. "Moon drove to Hattiesburg to try to console his mother. He said she's taking it well. Policeman's wife."

"I've heard," said John, "all kinds of stories about how and when Cory Morgan murdered him."

Nina shook her head:

"That's all they are: stories. We just know that after Cory's mother died he came here to clear his father's name. He was so bitter that murder didn't seem wrong to him. He was, like Jackson said about certain killers, on a mission from God. At any rate, he arrived in town about the same time Michael Yancy did. How Cory found out Michael had just been hired by Moon, who had not seen him since he was a small boy and would not recognize him, we don't know. We only know that Cory shot him in his motel room the night before he was to report. Even took his uniform, which he was wearing the morning he reported. No, he thought of everything, right down to shaving his head so that no one could tell he was red headed."

They ate for a time longer, speaking of this and that.

Frank appeared at the table, sat in an empty chair, smiled, and then disappeared.

He had been doing that a good deal on the chairs of Nina's deck, since her return from the hospital.

Hope, Nina could not help noting, was looking at the same chair.

Seeing, Nina knew, her Marshall.

They sipped their blood red wine, and listened to the ocean.

THE END

ABOUT THE AUTHORS

 Pam 'T'Gracie' Reese is an assistant professor of communication sciences and disorders at Indiana University-Purdue University Fort Wayne (IPFW). Nina Bannister was created while T'Gracie was a doctoral student at the University of Louisiana-Lafayette. She has happy memories of exploring Acadiana, dancing the Cajun waltz, catching beads at Mardi Gras and listening to French on the radio. (Geaux Cajuns!) Still, she also loves her new life in Ft. Wayne and enjoys getting to know northern Indiana. (Go Mastodons!)

Joe Reese is a writer and teacher. He's only partially responsible for the six Nina Bannister mysteries (co-written with his wife, T'Gracie), but he has to take full blame for *Kate Dee and Katie Haw: Letters from a Texas Farm Girl* and the play *Lunacy: A Play for Our Times*.

He and his wife have three children: Kate, Matthew, and Sam. The two of them now live in Fort Wayne, Indiana, where each teaches at IPFW.

www.ingramcontent.com/pod-product-compliance
Lightning Source LLC
Chambersburg PA
CBHW050413260626
47156CB00003B/986